A DEGREE OF FUTILITY

To Donald and Eve: 2014
Who understand discipline,
rigour and good humour!
M[illegible].

M.P. FEDUNKIW

First Edition – January 2014

Cover photograph by Matthew Ross, Springfed Creative

Author photograph by Marlis Funk, Imaging by Marlis

ISBN
978-1-4602-3379-5 (Hardcover)
978-1-4602-3380-1 (Paperback)
978-1-4602-3381-8 (eBook)

Produced by:

FriesenPress
Suite 300 – 852 Fort Street
Victoria, BC, Canada V8W 1H8

www.friesenpress.com

Distributed to the trade by The Ingram Book Company

To my dear friend,
gentle reader,
and fellow graduate student,
George Dutton

Vivat membrum quodlibet!

CHAPTER 1

Alma Mater floreat,	May our Alma Mater thrive,
Quae nos educavit;	That which educated us;
Caros et commilitones,	Dear ones and comrades,
Dissitas in regions	Whom we let scatter afar,
Sparsos, congregavit.	Let us assemble.

— *From 'Gaudeamus igitur',*
an early 18th century song based on a late
13th century Latin manuscript

May 2002

I was jolted out of a glorious slumber by my evil alarm clock. I silenced it with one blind slap. After a long night reviewing my dissertation, my eyeballs felt like a couple of dried raisins so before anything in the room could come into focus, I rolled them around in their sockets to lube them up. Then I glanced at the clock. It read five after eight. That was cutting it close even though I did live near the campus.

I had just thrown off the covers to swing my legs over the edge of the bed when the phone rang.

"Who the hell?" I lunged across the bed to pick it up. "Hello?"

"Good morning, soon-to-be Dr. Halton."

"Simon?"

"Of course. Who else rings you from abroad?"

"Only you, Dr. Beale."

"Are you awake?" he asked.

"Of course I'm awake."

"You just awakened."

"What?"

"I can hear it in your voice. You always over enunciate when you're trying to let on that you've been awake for hours. Better get used to getting up, my dear. Your days as a student are almost over."

"That's if I pass."

"You'll do just fine, Lily."

"Christ, Simon, why did I have to draw a nine o'clock defense? You know I'm crap in the morning."

"Blame the mad, mad world of university administration."

"Comforting."

"By noon, you'll be a free woman."

"You mean unemployed."

"Don't be so pessimistic. Worst case, you may be underemployed for a bit. Look at it this way. You're starting the next phase of your life, combing the internet for interesting postdocs in fascinating places. Maybe even a stunning tenure-track position right away, somewhere Greg and I can visit often."

I glanced at the clock. "It's almost eight thirty. I've got to get in the shower."

"Go. Perform thy ablutions. I simply wanted to make sure you didn't sleep through your own exam. "

"Thanks. I hope I can say the same about my supervisor."

"You'll be free of that silly old sod in a few hours, too."

"He'll still have to write me reference letters."

"Of course, but your world is about to widen like you never dreamed of, El." For years, Simon had affectionately called me by my first initial, especially when he was trying to impart his wisdom. I tried calling him 'Es', but that never took because everyone misunderstood and thought I was calling him esquire, which he loved and I loathed.

I sighed. "I am so glad that you finished before me. You're my road map."

"Then you are doomed," he said. "In any case, good luck, have fun and remember, you know more about films as a public health tool in the first half of the twentieth century than anyone else. You are the expert. So go forth and impress. Ring me later."

"I will. Thanks." I hung up and rushed to the shower.

Simon was one of my two best friends. Greg was the other. We all met seven years ago when we enrolled in the Master's program at the History of Science, Medicine and Technology Institute at University of Toronto. There were seven students in our class: Maggie, whose background was in environmental science and who had worked in South America for a few years for various NGOs; Janice, who had done her first degree in medical genetics at Rutgers; Louis, an odd fellow who was obsessed with the taxonomy of fish; Max, the budding microbiologist; Greg, who arrived with a Bachelor's of Business Administration to please his father and wanted to study Frederick Taylor's models for increasing efficiency in technological systems; Simon, from Cambridge, who arrived with a paper on Newton already published in a leading academic journal; and me. Four of us decided to stay on for the PhD; Simon, Greg, Max and me.

Max only lasted two years before switching over to medical school because he saw better career options open to him as a physician.

I didn't like Simon when we first met. He was brilliant, English, an only child, gay, and pretentious, and I sensed he was always mocking me. It didn't help that in a quasi-competitive environment, his deck was stacked because his parents, now dead, had been renowned academics. He grew up knowing the ropes.

Everything seemed to come easily to him. I put it down to the being English thing and already having a Cambridge degree. But then, over the course of the two-year MA, I discovered that although he was a bit posh – his own self-deprecating description – he was also generous. If anyone was a bit tight for money, he would discreetly make things right. If someone was stuck on their dissertation, Simon would do whatever was needed to help them along, either by reading a draft, talking through the problem or suggesting possible sources. He was such a natural at the whole academic lifestyle that anyone who hung around with him was bound to learn something by osmosis.

Greg was, in many ways, Simon's academic opposite. He'd worked in an automobile plant to put himself through his undergraduate degree and decided to go back to school against his father's wishes. His father wouldn't even come to his MA convocation. "Stupid smart ass," his dad called him. "Think you're better than everyone else? And you won't even be a *real* doctor if you finish."

Greg found graduate school challenging but he had a fantastic work ethic. When I asked him what motivated him, he said during high school he'd been a solid B-minus student and had to work at all things academic. "I'm a plodder," he said. "But at least I know that up front. Everyone can't be a genius like Simon."

As I showered, I had one of those flashbacks that reviewed my entire graduate student career like the images movies show the moment before someone dies. Through it all, Greg and Simon were there to motivate me, to make me laugh, and to encourage me to keep at it. So many times I wondered if I would make it, not because I thought I wasn't good enough or bright enough. Writing a dissertation is a slog. You really have to love your topic because no one cares if you finish. No wonder so many students lose momentum and quit.

I stepped out of the shower and toweled off. Catching a glimpse of myself in the mirror, it struck me that today was one of those days when everything would change. If the exam went well, I would be Dr. Halton. My library card would be good until the end of the month and then I'd be cut loose. But I had to get through this exam first. I went over to the stereo and popped in a CD with dance tunes to work off my nervous energy as I dressed in clothes I'd set out the night before.

My supervisor kept telling me today would be the last time anyone was paid to read my work; after this, I'd have to earn their attention. Professor Hamish MacPhee was a good supervisor from the point of view of being a prolific scholar who had published five monographs, three edited volumes and more than fifty articles and countless book reviews in his forty-year career. As a supervisor, however, he was crap. I didn't want or need someone who would micro-manage my research, but MacPhee was so *laissez-faire* that in the last eighteen months of my writing up, when things were getting really tense, he was a non-entity. He either forgot scheduled meetings or showed up an hour late. Twice he lost chapters I gave him to read. By the end of the process, I wondered what the hell I was getting for my five thousand dollars in annual tuition other than an expensive library card.

Today was the culmination of years of work. I was looking forward to starting, as Simon said, the next phase of my life, so I gathered up a copy of my two hundred forty-five page dissertation and locked the door. I had an illogical and uneasy feeling of impending doom that I put down to lack of sleep.

CHAPTER 2

WHEN I GOT TO THE EXAM ROOM WHERE I WOULD SPEND THE next few hours defending my dissertation, everyone was there except MacPhee. Five faculty members were chatting amicably and I sat down to silently review my notes when MacPhee waltzed in. When the chairperson glanced at his watch, MacPhee joked, "Am I late? I thought it was nine o'clock on U of T time." Classes started at ten past the hour so MacPhee thought he was being witty. I stifled a groan. The sooner my academic umbilical cord was cut, the better.

The examination began. The chair made sure that no one was long-winded and the time flew by. After everyone had asked their second question, I was asked to leave the room while they deliberated on one of three possible results: pass with distinction with the dissertation needing no amendments; pass with minor corrections; and pass with major revisions. I was left sitting alone on an upholstered bench seat contemplating which one was the likeliest outcome when I heard rustling. Leaning over to check the door of the exam room, I saw nothing. Again, I heard the sound of papers being rifled. I got up and walked along the deserted corridor to the top of the stairs. I jumped when I saw Greg sitting on the landing. He had all my course notes and was taking all the papers out of their three-ring binders.

"What the hell are you doing?"

"Getting ready to celebrate."

"They haven't told me I passed yet."

"It's only a matter of time."

"Well, they're taking a hell of a lot of time," I said, looking at my watch. "They've been in there for almost twenty minutes."

"Oh, you know MacPhee. He's probably kissing up to someone else on the committee or boring them with some story about his last conference."

"Maybe, but what if they really are anti-film and don't acknowledge the role of film as a primary source?"

"Calm down, Lil. You'll be fine. Simon liked your chapters, didn't he?"

"Yeah, he did."

"And he's the most conservative of them all, isn't he?"

"Yeah."

"So stop worrying."

I nodded at the pile of papers at his feet. "So what's with all my notes?"

"Oh," Greg said. "I figured when they came out to tell you that you'd passed, you and I could celebrate by burning all this course shit."

"Burn it here?"

"No silly, in your fireplace."

"Sounds good," I said, looking down at the growing mound of loose leaf paper. "Hard to believe we read and wrote this much, eh?"

"If anyone asks me what grad school taught me, I'd say how to perfect the art of sleeping with my eyes open."

I laughed. "I hear you. I also learned at least fifty new ways to procrastinate."

"What's your best?"

"Easy. One time, I just couldn't start a chapter so I got up and cleaned, by hand, all fifty-six bottles in my spice cabinet, including the empties."

"I wish I could be that productive," he said. "Best I can do is veg in front of the TV watching really bad re-runs. Or play my guitar till my fingers bleed, which means I can't type for a few more days."

"Speaking of music, remember the time you and Simon came over to my place and we wrote that full-length musical parody of the department?"

Greg smiled. "Sure. Remember that skit we did? The Dating Game with Newton, Marconi and Watson."

"Why was an entire show so easy to write by comparison?"

"If we could put dissertations to music it would be a hell of lot more fun."

"Or if we could collaborate. That was so much fun working with both of you," I said. "Maybe we should have done science PhDs and all worked in the same lab, eh?"

Greg sighed. "I'm going to miss you. It sucks being the one left behind."

I got up and sat beside him on the stair, taking care not to trip on the papers. "I know."

"With all due respect, Lil, you don't know. You and Simon are top of the class. Probably have been since kindergarten. All I've got going for me is persistence."

"That seems to count for a lot in the academic game."

"We'll see," he said.

"Remember the fun we had writing those songs? Do you think anyone will ever remember that stuff?"

"I know a few people who will never be able to look at you without seeing you in that bustier wielding that whip."

"Stop it," I said.

"You looked hot. One prof asked where we got our costumes but I know he cared only about your dominatrix costume."

"Work my ass off for five years, bury myself in moldy films and dusty articles to write my *magnum opus*, and I'm remembered for a black bustier?"

"Stranger things have led to full-time jobs, I'm told," he said with a grin.

I leaned over to punch him in the arm. "You are such a ..."

"Guy?"

"That wasn't the first word that came to mind."

"So shoot me for being a man first and a scholar second," he said rubbing his arm.

"*Touché*!"

We sat for a minute before Greg broke the silence. "It seems like yesterday that I sat down next to you, that first day, in the Common Room, for our MA orientation."

"I was still working full-time that first week."

"I still wonder if you, me, or even Simon could have made it doing something even more dramatic, more ... out there."

"Like what, Greg?"

"We can always try writing a sequel to that departmental parody and try to reach a wider audience. All we need is one lucky break," he said.

"And good material."

"The academic life, idiosyncratic profs, those theories and ideas. Lil, the material is so juicy, it would be a cake walk," Greg said. "Remember that philandering lounge lizard, the one who parted his seven hairs eight different ways?"

"Or the one who wore slippers to lectures and always carried bits of lunch in his mangy old beard." We were both howling now and I didn't hear the committee chair walking down the hall.

"Ms. Halton?"

It was only when I heard his deep voice that I noticed the tips of worn brogues on the edge of the top stair.

I struggled to compose myself as I watched the Chair take in the chaos of papers and Greg draped across the stairs.

"Yes. I'm sorry. Shall I come back in now?"

"Please," he said. "And may I be the first to congratulate you?" He extended his hand.

"Really?"

He smiled. "Uh-huh. Really!"

"Told you so," said Greg.

I walked back down the long corridor with the Chair.

"Your boyfriend looked pleased," he said after a few steps in silence.

"Oh, he's not my boyfriend. We started the program together."

"Was that his dissertation he was sorting through?"

I laughed. "Not at all."

"Well, in any case, your friend seemed genuinely happy for you."

"It seemed like the committee was deliberating a while. I thought it was taking so long because something was drastically wrong."

"No, nothing like that." He chuckled. "Your supervisor is quite the raconteur. He spins an amusing, albeit lengthy, yarn."

"Yes." What else could I say?

We had arrived at the door and I could hear the group chatting. The Chair paused with his hand on the doorknob. "So after you've completed the corrections to your manuscript, what will you do next?"

I had no idea.

CHAPTER 3

AS I WALKED OUT OF THE ROOM, MY ARMS ACHED UNDER THE weight of more than fifteen hundred manuscript pages. I tried to shift the bundles to even out the weight but my efforts had the opposite effect.

"Help!" I waited a second as the mountain of papers began to slip. "Greg?"

"Yes, Dr. Halton," he said from the staircase.

"Come here."

When he saw me struggling, he ran to me with my course notes under one arm.

"Jeezus, Lily. Why didn't you ask me to help?"

"I thought I did, you knob."

"I mean, you should've told me to bring a box and I would have packed them up when you were ready."

"Yeah, well, I didn't think that far ahead. I forget that all the committee members would give me their copies, all marked up. Hey, at least you'll know for your exam."

"Sure."

I smiled. "I'm your training wheels."

"What?"

"Use me. And my experience"

"Sounds kinky," he said.

"Does everything come back to sex for you?"

He shrugged. "Call me an optimist."

I held the door open for him as he effortlessly balanced the paper bundles on his shoulders.

"Happy?" he asked.

"I'm exhausted."

"Why don't you go home and take a nap? I'll be here working. Call me when you wake up and we can meet up and go for dinner."

"I thought we were going to burn my notes."

"There'll be time for that. Go home and rest," he said. "Where do you want me to drop all this?"

"I just thought I'd leave it in my carrel. No need to put it in the main office. No one's going to steal it. I'll worry about lugging it home later."

"Your wish is my command, madam. I mean doctor."

I feigned haughtiness. "Oh, mere plebian. Because you knew me before I attained that lofty and deserved title, you may address me less formally."

"As smarty bitch?"

"That's Madam Smarty Bitch to you!"

I was going to miss this. I loved the easy banter. Greg was closer to me than my own sisters and brothers. He understood me. If Greg knew my heart, Simon understood my head. Simon had left for Oxford the previous September. Now I would have to move on to the next phase of my career, leaving Greg to catch up.

"Thanks," I said. And I went home. It felt so good to change out of my suit, slip out of the blouse, roll down the nylons I hated, and flop on the bed. I think I was asleep before my head hit the pillow and I slept like a log, despite the streetcars clanging outside and the light streaming through my window. I hadn't set an alarm so when I woke up I was shocked to see that I'd slept for hours. It was just after five.

I got up and looked in the mirror at a face that was covered with a map of haphazard creases from the pillow.

"Hey there, Doctor. You look like hell!"

I showered, put on a comfortable shirt and my best jeans. I heard my stomach grumbling. Walking to the refrigerator, I contemplated whether I should eat and ruin dinner or risk passing out from low blood sugar. Opening the fridge, the decision was made for me. It was almost empty. I took out some milk, went to the cupboard for some cereal and sat down at the kitchen table to have my second breakfast of the day. When I'd finished, I rinsed out the melamine bowl, washed the spoon and picked up the phone. He picked up after two rings.

"Hi."

"Did you sleep?" he asked.

"Like the dead."

"Ready for dinner?"

"You bet."

"Okay," he said. "Come by and we can decide where we want to go."

"Great. Oh, can you meet me downstairs?"

"Sure. Why?"

"I wanted to bring some boxes so I can slowly pack up my stuff."

"You can't wait to get out, eh?"

"No," I said. "But I'd rather leave on my schedule instead of being booted out."

"Yeah, I get it. Call me when you're downstairs and I'll help you."

I hung up and finished getting ready. On the way to the university I stopped at the local grocery store and picked up five sturdy boxes. Standing on the edge of the street, I hailed a cab, loaded some boxes in the trunk and tossed two in the back seat before climbing in myself.

"Moving, miss?" the cabbie asked, glancing in his rearview mirror.

"Out of my office."

He nodded. "Small office."

"I just passed my doctoral exam. One minute I'm a grad student. The next minute, an unemployed person."

He chuckled. "Do you want to drive a taxi?"

"God, no!" I said then felt obliged to soften the exclamation. "I mean, I don't like driving that much."

"Sure. I don't like it much either. I finished my PhD back home."

"Where's home?"

"India. I was teaching at the local university but then decided to bring my family here for a better life for my kids. But there are no jobs for me here in Toronto. Not in my field. I should have listened to my father and taken engineering, but I loved poetry."

"That's tough," I said.

"So after looking for a few months, I had to take a job, any job, to pay the bills. And so now I'm a taxi man." We stopped at a red light on Bay Street and he turned his head around to face me. "What field did you choose?"

I felt a tingle in my stomach before I spoke. "History of medicine."

"So you are not a medical doctor?"

"No."

"Well," he sighed. "I hope you have better luck. Engineers, doctors even undertakers, they will always find work in their fields. But for those of us who love literature, history and the rest of the humanities, I fear that until the world begins to appreciate the arts again, we will have to be very resourceful to survive."

The light turned green and we were off again. I couldn't believe I was hearing this lecture on the day I had defended. He drove me almost to the door of the building and helped me unload the boxes. I found a ten-dollar bill to pay the eight dollar fare and pulled out a loonie to give him a generous tip. It was shitty to be an immigrant intellectual with no job in his field. I noticed flecks of grey in his sideburns but otherwise he looked to be about my age, maybe a few years older.

He put out his hand to shake mine. "Good luck, miss."

I thanked him and he was off. As the taxi disappeared along Charles Street, I pulled out my cell phone and called Greg, empty boxes at my feet.

"I'm downstairs, Greg."

"I'll be right down." He was there in a flash.

As we waited for the creaky old elevator, Greg balanced the boxes like a circus juggler on one knee.

"So, minor corrections?"

"Yup."

"Are you pissed?"

"Nah," I said. "Simon is the first person in thirty years to finish with distinction, so I figure I'm doing well if I get the silver medal."

"I overheard one prof in the men's washroom say that he thought Simon was brilliant," Greg said.

I laughed. "I'm sure Simon would agree with you."

"I dared him to submit leather bound copies to his committee to save time."

"You're such a shit."

"Do you miss your topic yet?" Greg asked.

"Not yet. I was so sick of the thing by the time I'd submitted, I never did a really good final copyediting."

"You should have asked me."

"I didn't want to pull you away from your work."

"Hell, copyediting would have been entertainment for me, especially when I was bogged down in pissy little footnotes."

"Yeah but now they're done, right?"

"Right." The elevator jerked to a stop at the third floor.

We walked to the door of the common room and I pulled out my key to open the door. The old wooden door with the opaque glass panel swung open to hoots and hollers.

"What the ... ?"

Greg grinned. "It's your last grad party, Lil."

CHAPTER 4

ALL THE GRADUATE STUDENTS FROM THE INSTITUTE WERE THERE as well as some of the faculty. The drinking had obviously begun before we'd arrived and it took less than a minute before a glass of wine was pressed into my hand. Greg had put the boxes out of harm's way and came back with a beer.

"Relax," he said. "Tomorrow, the work will still be here, but tonight savour the fact that you beat the odds."

I hugged him. "Thanks. You're the best!"

"Don't you forget it."

"I promise." Then I was swept up in a stream of hugs and congratulations. MacPhee, to his credit, came over to shake my hand.

"Well done, Lily!" he said. "You've done an admirable job of raising the reputation of film as a legitimate academic source."

It was so like him to damn with faint praise. Still on my first glass of wine, I fought back the urge to tell him what I really thought of the space he took up as a full faculty member, and I simply thanked him.

Greg broke away from the students he'd been talking with and moved to the centre of the room. Picking up a metal serving spoon from the potluck table, he tapped it against his beer bottle. When the buzz of many conversations died down, he spoke.

"We are gathered here today ... Shit! I sound like a minister!"

Everyone laughed.

"Seriously, we're here to celebrate the successful defense of Lily, who will pretty soon be *Doctor* Halton. As happy as she probably is at a time like this, I'm sure she, and *some* of us, is missing our good friend and favourite pain in the ass, Simon. So, even though I don't have Simon's posh accent or huge vocabulary, I'd like to offer a few words of wisdom as he might, by offering up a metaphor. But first ..."

Then he dipped one hand into the back pocket of his jeans and pulled out a serviette. He opened it up, deftly folded it in half so that he had a large triangle and then tucked it into his opened necked shirt like a quasi-ascot.

"Ahem. Now for the metaphor," he said before pausing to draw a long breath. "We are all sailing on the Sea of Higher Knowledge, each of us in our own small boat." He smiled as many groaned. "Some have just set off and, glancing back, can see *terra firma* – that's Latin for 'land'. Some are on the open ocean where everyone thinks about either turning back or leaping out." He smiled. "If they say they don't, they're lying."

"Then there's Lily, who is within sight of her destination. She can see all the profs on the tropical Isle of Tenure, comfy in their tweed and corduroy bathing suits, sipping sherry and piña coladas, secure in the fact that no matter how badly they teach or how boring their writing may be, no one can boot them off the island." He glanced at the profs huddled together in one corner and shrugged. "Sorry. Just channeling Simon."

He turned to look at me. "Today is the first day you can raise your head above your computer keyboard and think about your future,

Lily." Raising his beer, he continued, "We, the friends you're leaving behind, wish you success, adventure and good, sane colleagues. Simon gave me another Latin phrase to end with, but I've forgotten it, so … *e pluribus unum*!"

"Your Latin is getting much better, Greg," I said.

He smiled. Then everyone started clapping and yelling 'Speech!' I put down my wine and took a breath before I spoke.

"It's still sinking in," I said. "Doing a PhD has been like climbing a mountain. While I was mired in the material, I couldn't see the end or remember where I'd started. But one page at a time, the manuscript grew. Something made me keep going. Part of it was the fact that I loved my topic. Part of it was having Greg and Simon kicking me when I stalled. And this room always offered a respite from the work. Whether it was talking about a chapter or just laughing over something stupid, this room, you guys, sustained me. I know it sounds like AA … Hey, maybe we should start a branch of another AA – Academics Anonymous. Anyway, thanks for the party. I really appreciate it!" I paused for a moment before adding, "Oh yeah. I'm not going anywhere right now, so even if they take away my keys, please let me into the Common Room."

Everyone clapped and with the speeches over, the party was now in full swing. It felt so good to relax, to catch up with people whom I had neglected in the run-up to the exam, and not to feel guilty about ignoring my writing. Someone slipped a dance CD into the stereo and suddenly the party turned into two parties. Those who wanted to talk went out into the hallway and the rest of us who loved to dance kicked off our shoes.

I glanced through the crowd to catch Greg's eyes. He smiled and raised his beer. His shirt was now stuck to his lean body because it was warm on the third floor and the century-old building had no central air conditioning. I could feel droplets of perspiration and they sat, poised for a second just above the cleft between my breasts before they broke away to race towards my belly. The back of my shirt clung to my skin and if I had been more adventurous, I might have reached in to unhook my bra and toss it aside. Inhibitions? What inhibitions? I suddenly remembered the day I was trying to pay Greg some money I owed him. I took twenty dollars out of my pocket and held it out to him.

"What's that for?" he asked.

"Earlier this week you loaned me twenty bucks for dinner. Remember?"

"That's okay."

"Nope, I pay my debts."

"It's fine. You can pick up the tab next time."

"What if I'm hit by a streetcar?"

"I'll chalk it up to a bad debt."

I shrugged. "I'll keep it in the bank then," I said as I folded up the bill and slipped it down my top into my bra.

"Really?" he asked grinning.

"For safekeeping."

"What if I want to make a withdrawal?"

"You can make one any time."

"Really?"

"Yup."

"If I changed my mind and needed that twenty now?"

I knew him. Greg talked a good game with the ladies but was never one to make the first move, so I took a step closer and stuck my chest out.

"Come and get it," I said.

That's when I learned something new about my friend. No sooner had I thrown down the gauntlet then he calmly came toward me and, with consummate ease, slipped his hand down my shirt, grasped the bill and pulled it out.

"All this and no bank fees, eh?"

I was still standing there, feet rooted to the floor, speechless.

"Lil?"

"I can't believe ... you ... you ..."

"You forgot business was my undergrad degree. Supply and demand. You supplied the goods and demanded I try." He winked.

I remembered feeling the colour rise in my cheeks, just like I could now, but this time it was likely due to too much wine. So when the first few notes of the next dance tune started and Greg walked across the room, I was hot, flushed, feeling sentimental and keen to dance with my best friend.

"Howdy, sailor," I began.

"Don't you mean, 'Howdy, scholar?'" Greg put his hands out to take mine.

"Don't know how well that works."

"As what? A pick-up line?"

"I didn't think I had to pick you up," I said.

"Aren't *we* sure of ourselves this evening!"

I laughed. "The 'h' in PhD stands for hubris."

"And what if I played hard to get?"

"Well, I've never chased a guy in my life, and I'm not going to start now."

He picked me up and swung me around.

"Greg, put me down," I said, laughing.

"I'm going to twirl some sense into you, woman."

My feet were still in the air.

"You're going to twirl something out of me, that's for sure, but it ain't gonna be pretty if you don't stop soon."

He laughed as he slowed down and my feet came to rest on the floor. My head, however, continued to spin so I was holding on to his shoulders to keep my balance.

"Lil?"

"Yeah?"

"We're not dancing anymore."

"Speak for yourself. My feet may not be moving but my stomach is still doing pirouettes."

"You can lean on me whenever and for as long as you want."

I tilted my head up to look at him. We'd been friends for years yet this was the first time I'd really looked at him. His brown curls were moist with sweat just behind his ears. He wore his hair long, not out of a sense of style but out of neglect. One of the joys of being a graduate student was that no one really cared if you kept up with style.

The Beau Brummel in our circle was Simon. He was at least six foot two with long legs. Bow ties, three-button blazers, coloured shirts and shoes that were always polished as if he were an army officer. Simon also loved to sculpt his facial hair – one month growing and grooming a Van Dyke, then wide sideburns closely cropped to his face, followed by a neat little soul patch a few months later. It helped that he had fantastic bone structure, with a sleek Roman nose, high cheekbones and a wonderful head of dark blond hair that framed his face so well.

Greg was handsome, too, but in a different way. He was shorter than Simon and his build was stockier, too. But his eyes lit up whenever he began to smile and he radiated a quiet warmth and reassurance that I realized I had taken for granted all these years. I would never have called Greg sexy. He was comfortable, the kind of guy a girl could count on. He had dated a couple of women since starting grad school, but neither of them seemed to sustain him intellectually and he let the relationships dim until both women left. No fuss. No histrionics.

"Lil? You all right?"

"Sure. Sure. I'm fine."

"Not that I'm complaining," he said, a slow smile creeping across his face.

I reached up to push a lock of hair that had flopped over one eye out of his eye.

"Who's going to do that?" he asked.

"What?"

"Take care of me," he replied.

"Take care of you? Mr. Independent?" I swatted him. He was still holding on to me, music blaring, others dancing around us.

"Okay. Who's going to keep an eye on *you* if you go away?"

"Like the absent-minded dumb-ass I am, I haven't applied for any jobs or postdocs yet, in Toronto or anywhere else, so don't get ahead of yourself."

"I just worry," he said.

"About what?"

"What's going to happen to us?"

I shook my head. "Right now, I'm going to get another drink. Then I'm going to dance until someone kicks us out of here. I'll worry about my future tomorrow. And you're so close to finishing that maybe we can swing getting jobs in the same city or at least cities that are close."

Greg shrugged. He was no longer touching me, but his brown eyes were still fixed on me. "Your stomach feeling better?"

I was suddenly aware of how intense the last few minutes had been and I was feeling a bit uneasy. This was supposed to be a party. "Yeah, thanks," I said before I gave him a quick peck on the cheek. "You'll make someone a wonderful mother one day!" And then I went back into the Common Room to get something to quench my thirst.

As I turned the door handle, I glanced back at Greg who stood, looking a tad forlorn, before a young MA student, obviously smitten, sidled up to him. He looked over at me. I winked and he shrugged his shoulders before putting out one hand to accept the dance.

Just then it hit me that I'd promised to call Simon. I checked my watch. It would be after five in Cambridge. I poured myself a glass of wine and sneaked out of the Common Room to the main office where it was quieter. As I dialled, I could still hear the music seeping under the wide gap of the closed door. The phone rang four or five times before he picked up.

"Hello?"

"Is this the renowned and supercilious Simon Beale?"

"The very same. Might this be the petulantly ambitious Lily Halton?"

"It is, indeed."

There was a moment of silence. "Well …," he drew out in his deepest baritone.

"Despite my punctually challenged supervisor and one committee member who kept falling asleep, they decided, in their wisdom, to allow me to join their ranks."

"Bravo, old girl!"

I laughed. "Ah Simon, I can always count on you to make me feel just that. Old."

"Don't be ridiculous, El. You just started later in life than some of us. Left the dark side to bask in the lonely but intellectually unrivalled world of esoteric research."

"You make it sound so romantic."

"You'll see," he said. "Guess how I spent my day?"

"Sanctimoniously?"

He laughed. "Cheeky girl. That's why I adore you. I had tea with one of the curators at the Whipple. He's working on a paper comparing the materials used in Eastern and Western astrolabes. We spent more than an hour perusing various pieces, including a silver celestial planisphere in their Holden-White Collection, circa 1700."

"I thought you were working on Newton?"

"Oh El, you're still thinking like a constrained graduate student. Of course my main focus is still Newton. But being back in Cambridge for a few days, it would have been a travesty not to immerse myself in other fascinating intellectual diversions, just for the bloody fun of it. Think of it as a pedagogical *amuse bouche*."

"I guess."

He sighed. "You'll see. So what's next?"

"Simon, I don't have any firm plans yet. It took all my focus to finish the diss."

"Well, madam. Finish that glass of wine I know you're holding and go home and start combing H-Net for interesting prospects."

I chuckled. "You are an uncanny judge of behaviour."

"It is both my curse and my burden," he said. "By the way, how's our boy holding up?"

"Greg?"

"Who else?"

"He's his usual kind and helpful self."

"I should guess a tad morose, too."

"He's worried about being abandoned," I said.

"Well, you could always make his day, consummate the relationship and take him with."

"Ah Simon, cut me some slack."

"You know he's been infatuated with you since our first day."

"I didn't do anything to encourage him. You know that."

"Vile seductress."

"Right."

"The Fates will take care of things as they see fit. Before I ring off, I promise I shall raise a glass of vintage port to you this evening at High Table. And consider yourself forewarned -- I shall give you a fortnight to compile your list of prospective future employers before I come to your rescue and counsel you in the *proper* direction. Best to Master Gregory. This evening you can sleep the sleep of the erudite and the just!"

"Thanks, you pompous old ass."

"Pompous, perhaps, but I shall always be younger than you, my dear." He rang off.

Sitting on the edge of the desk, I smiled. As I got up to pull the chain on the lamp that dimly lit the office, I got the feeling I was going to need both Simon and Greg even more now that I was off the PhD grid and stepping off into the chasm that was the job search.

CHAPTER 5

WHAT BUOYED ME UP THAT YEAR, IN ADDITION TO HEARING stories of the fascinating work that Simon was doing and Greg's gentle prodding, was the realization that few people in the world have the opportunity to spend their lives pursuing a question that intrigues them. Doctors don't get to choose their patients. Teachers don't teach only the kids they like. Undertakers don't get to select the corpses they prepare and bury.

Academic freedom was the seductive ideal that drew me back to university when I turned twenty-eight. I had been working for five years at a large public relations firm in Toronto. At first the work was exciting and challenging. I loved that projects changed frequently; the travel was fantastic; and being ambitious, I was given larger projects to manage. The team I supervised was terrific. We were all around the same age and spent many late nights in the office refining ideas, then celebrating at the pub around the corner. The money was great and I moved into a swish waterfront condo. My life was made.

But sometime during the third year, I began to want more. Not more money. Not even, I surprised myself, a better position. When

I asked myself the question, 'Where do I see myself in five or ten years?' I had this nagging idea that writing briefs and stellar memos for thousands of dollars was not making the best use of my intellect and imagination.

I was also coming to notice that my colleagues and I were different. They reveled in climbing the corporate ladder and each business triumph. They were sharp, keen and hungry for more of the same, every day. They were also efficient and read only books that might get them ahead in their careers. Long after I'd left university, I was still reading widely, often esoteric academic non-fiction with no connection to business, management studies or team building.

Just after I'd been at the firm for four years, I started a relationship with one of the senior VPs from another firm. Oliver was almost thirty years older than me, charming, erudite and he met my need for a mentor. We met at a conference. The attraction was fierce; we were in bed together within the first month of his moving to Toronto from the London office. He was divorced with children older than me, so he had copious amounts of time and money to seduce me with dinners at Scaramouche, cocktails at The Sutton Place Hotel, and theatre trips to New York City.

I'd never been in a relationship with someone like Oliver. There were times I felt I was living a dream. I fell in love with his tailored navy chalk-stripe suits and custom-made shirts. When we went to an opera gala, he wore his own dinner jacket and tied his own bow tie. He spoke French and Italian fluently and cooked meals like a chef. He was irresistibly sexy, his dark hair peppered with silver, kept just a bit longer so that it teased his collar. I loved going back to his condo in Yorkville after a formal event, clutching and grabbing at each other like a pair of randy teenagers even as he deftly managed to slip his key into the lock, then reaching up to loop my finger around one end of the bow tie and, with a smart tug, blowing it open just like in a sixties spy film.

Sunday mornings were spent in bed reading *The New York Times* with a simple brunch of fresh squeezed orange juice, *pain au chocolat* and Bodum press coffee. I loved sitting with him, naked under a feather duvet, propped up on a mound of oversized pillows. He was sexiest peering over his bifocals at me as we chatted about what we'd been reading. I couldn't believe I was being pampered by a man who was already an executive when I was born. The age difference was never an issue between us but I was aware that we got looks from some people when we walked, hand in hand. I loved the fact that he treated me so well, that he never tired of my discussions about my future or helping me understand the business we were both in.

Oliver seemed honestly keen to share a lifetime's experience with me, although we came from different worlds. Not simply the fact that he was British and I was born in Toronto, or that he'd been educated at public school followed by Oxford University. The only time we ever disagreed was more an issue of what he called focus. By the time we started our relationship, I was questioning if a career in public relations was the way I wanted to spend my working life. Oliver had been committed to success in business from the time he finished at Oxford. He did not waver. His was a steady climb facilitated by both what he knew and those whom he knew. I sensed the fact that he enjoyed being my Svengali, as he jokingly called himself, and that my success would gratify his ego, too. So when, one Sunday morning like so many before, we lay in bed after making love, I mentioned going to graduate school, I was shocked by his reply.

"That urge will pass, dearest," he said while stroking my hair.

My curiosity was piqued. "Why?"

"Oh, every intelligent person yearns for greater challenges when they've been at it for a few years."

"Did you?"

He laughed. "Of course. I wanted to return to the warm bosom of academe to study Ovid and Homer."

"Why?"

"I was in line for a directorship. I was very good at what I did, but I was frustrated by a colleague who was trying to thwart my rise within the company. He was giving me only secondary projects, burying me under petty bureaucracy. The projects were not challenging at all and I questioned wasting more time when I thought I could do much more. I liked the firm. I didn't want to go over to a competitor but I pined for the intellectual stimulation I'd had at Oxford and thought seriously about returning for an advanced degree."

As I lay in bed, in the crook of his arm, I nodded. "What changed your mind?"

"Good sense. I realized that my path to success in the business would be blocked at times, but I had faith both in myself and that my work would be recognized. The nice thing about business is excellence is rewarded, even if it takes a bit of time, primarily because it's keyed to profit. And when I really thought long and hard about it, academia could never compare when it came to lifestyle."

"No," I said. "But a life spent in a university setting offers other benefits."

"Such as?"

"The independence to research whatever you like."

"And to live like a pauper."

"For the first few years."

"For the first decade, darling."

"Well, money isn't everything."

He peered over his bifocals at me. God, it was hard to resist his blue-grey eyes. "Would you give all this up and adore me more if this were an unheated garret? No more impromptu flights to New York City. No more posh dinners."

I had to admit I was torn. I wasn't asking him to go back to university. I really was convinced, however, that I could have my cake and eat it, too.

He sat upright and looked straight at me. "I get the sense we aren't really talking about philosophical stances regarding how one gets one's fulfillment in life, are we Lily?"

I pulled myself up, tucking my legs under my bare bottom so that I was almost level with him, chastely pulling up the duvet, too.

"Are you thinking of chucking your career to return to uni?" he asked.

I wasn't going to lie to my lover. "Yes."

He laughed and it stung. "My darling, that's madness. You're well on your way to …"

"To a life of professional boredom."

"Be patient."

"And wait for what?"

"For your promotion," he said, stroking my neck, but I flinched and he stopped.

"And then what?"

"Well, that depends on you, now doesn't it?"

I was seething. In a split second my charming lover had become a paternalistic and condescending ass.

"I'm good at what I do," I said.

"I know," he purred as he slipped his hand under the duvet and traced the curve from my breast to my hip, but I paid no attention to his *double entendre*.

"But it doesn't mean anything to me anymore."

"It did once, didn't it?"

I waved off his comment. "Of course, but when I extrapolate from where I am now, all I see is more of the same or managing more of the same. Sure, more money and better positions, but I want my working life to be more than fleeting projects and closing deals. I want to create something, add something to the world."

"You can do that later with philanthropy. Support the arts," he said. "I do."

"I want to contribute, to be part of the arts!"

He shook his head. "There's no guarantee there will be a job for you when you finish, you must realize that."

"If I'm good, I'll succeed."

Oliver sighed. "That works in business, ninety-nine percent of the time. But other factors drive university appointments."

"Such as?"

"Unpredictable factors, as well as predictable ones."

"Fine, Mr. Omniscient. Enlighten me."

"Well, when I was at Oxford it took little time for me to notice that although the university accepts students from everywhere, the faculty members were almost all Oxbridge types."

"What do you mean?" I asked.

"Lily, if you don't have a DPhil from Cambridge or Oxford, or occasionally a PhD from Harvard will do, you won't get a position at Cambridge or Oxford."

"I haven't ruled out going overseas for my PhD," I said, half lying to save face.

"Then there are the numbers," he continued.

"The numbers?"

"Although education is not my area of specialty, I read the papers and it seems to me that faculty hires are not keeping pace with the need or the number of graduates."

I shrugged. "If I'm good ..."

"It might not be enough."

I rose up on my knees to peer down at him. "How can you be so singularly unsupportive?"

He looked up at me, dumbfounded. "Lily darling, I am supportive. I want you to shine. You've got a real future in business communications. You're on track for a senior directorship within the year with world travel, six figures and a chance to move up further soon after, but the academy is a whole different world. You'll be starting from scratch, toiling away alone, judged by senior scholars who may or may not care about you or your project. Going into debt if you're not lucky, scraping by if you are, then graduating into a market that promises to be among the most uncertain in recent memory. And if you can't make a go of it, you'll have lost valuable time on the executive track as well as hundreds of thousands of dollars in earnings."

"But what if I'm numb with boredom?"

Oliver laughed. "You've never been to an academic conference, I see."

"I'm serious."

He took my hand. "I am, too, darling. Of course I'll adore you whatever you choose, but don't be hasty. Think about it." He shifted closer. "Now, can we end this strategic session and spend the rest of the day exploring," he paused to caress my breast, "other things?"

The last thing I wanted to do was to make love, so I rolled away from Oliver, put on my robe and got into the shower. With warm water cascading down my face, I thought about everything he said. I got out of the shower, dressed and left Oliver's to return to my place. Alone, I reviewed my notes and various web pages to narrow down the programs I was most interested in.

That week, I applied for graduate school. To save money, I moved into a small apartment. Oliver and I continued our relationship but we argued more after I told him I'd been accepted, followed by more time spent in silence before I finally ended it with him. The last time I saw him I told him I couldn't be with someone who didn't understand me. He asked me to reconsider, but I needed to get out. I couldn't live in two worlds and he had no respect for the academic world I was now in.

Now, here I was, having completed the degree and once again perusing websites, but this time for fellowships and tenure-track jobs. Since my goal was a tenure-track job, I discounted short-term teaching positions, even if they were in Toronto. I had seen other new graduates get on that gerbil wheel and it rarely morphed into a tenured career. My other consideration was the fact that I didn't want to spend my life at a small Midwestern college somewhere in the US. I was a city person, so New York City, Chicago, San Francisco and Boston were really the only places I would look at south of the border. In Canada, I considered Vancouver, Edmonton, Toronto, Montreal and even Halifax, largely because those cities either had more than one university or a large research library.

At Simon's urging, and by his example, I was also willing to look at postdoctoral fellowships, but again at institutions in the top quartile worldwide. So I applied to Johns Hopkins, Harvard and Cornell in the US, Oxford and Cambridge in the UK, and my *alma mater*. I passed over at least twenty others in smaller locales or lesser universities because I figured that a first-rate postdoc would lead to a first-rate job, but a second-tier postdoc would limit me to second-rate posts at best.

I sent out six applications over the course of my last year, but got no nibbles. I chalked that up to bad timing and not yet having my degree in hand. Now it was different. Although I was now finished and no longer had to pay fees, I was no longer working as a research or teaching assistant. Rent still had to be paid and I thought it might be strategic to go to a few conferences to show people that I was on the job market, but the best conferences that year would include flights and hotels totaling a minimum of fifteen hundred dollars each.

So that year I went back to my old firm to see if there was some contract work available. Fortunately, many of my contacts were still there, but my former colleagues had used the past six years to move up in the organization. I ended up having coffee with one of my former team members, whom I had supervised. She was now a vice president. We had an interesting chat and she said she'd have her secretary call me that week.

The secretary did call and I got a project that lasted three months and replenished my account, funding one research trip to the National Library of Medicine in Washington, D.C., and paying my way to attend a pair of conferences in Vancouver and Boston. It was quite a contrast on these trips to stay in second-rate hotels to save money, packing a bowl and spoon to eat boxed cereal purchased at a corner store to avoid costly hotel breakfasts. When I was working full-time, the firm always put me up in first-rate hotels, with all the amenities needed to do business efficiently and well. If I needed a reality check, I had Simon and Greg.

But as fall faded into winter and winter turned to spring with only a collection of 'Fuck Off and Die', or FOAD, letters accumulating on my desk, my resolve was fading. Each day I spent combing the websites was eating away at my confidence. It didn't help that the academic job market was cyclical. Most jobs were posted in the late spring and early summer for that fall or the following year, with another burst of applications in the fall. The winter was typically a dead zone, which could stretch into April and early May.

As the year wore on and I had word of those hired, I also noticed that the hires often had little in common with the areas of research or qualifications listed in the original posting. I was getting more and more frustrated even as I was more puzzled.

I often thought of Oliver. I was going to hate it if he proved to be right.

CHAPTER 6

BY AUGUST, WITH NOTHING ON THE HORIZON, I WAS GOING CRAZY. Some nights I'd dream about meeting Oliver, having nothing to say when he'd ask what I was doing. In the worst of those dreams, he'd just laugh and laugh, and say, "Faculty hires are not keeping pace with the need."

Greg did his best to keep my spirits up. I should have been a better friend to him as he was trying to finish his own draft, but I was a mess. One day, he called just after I opened my latest FOAD letter.

"Hi Lil!"

I couldn't stop myself. "I'm such a loser," I said and started sobbing.

"What are you talking about?"

"I just got another letter."

"Jesus. I'm sorry."

"What am I going to do, Greg?"

"Blow your nose. I'll be right over." And he hung up.

True to his word, he was at my door within twenty minutes. Without speaking a word I threw my arms around his neck and bawled. Only when I'd run out of tears and lifted my head did I notice the wet patch on his shoulder. I was embarrassed.

"Oh, Greg, I'm sorry."

"Ah, it's nothin' ma'am," he said, smiling. "I can deal with a wet spot."

I laughed in spite of my dire situation. "One track, just one track, eh?"

"I call it being focused," he said as he handed me a tissue. "In case there's any more where that came from," and he pointed to his wet shirt.

"I think I'm bone dry. I cried when I read the damned letter. I cried before you came and, well ..." I made a futile attempt to dry his pale blue polo shirt.

"Don't worry, I won't catch cold or die from a little mucous."

"Hey, I didn't drool on you."

"No, I prefer to think you were finally drooling over me."

"Yeah, stud? Self-praise stinks."

Greg smiled. "Now that's the Lily I know and adore – tough and sassy!"

I flopped down on the worn two-seat *faux* leather couch that was the centre piece of my small living room. "That old Lily is lost, Greg. It's been a year, and nothing."

Greg reached over to pull a wooden chair closer. With a twist of his wrist, he turned it around, slung one leg over and folded his arms to rest his head on the back of the chair.

"What did Simon say?" he asked.

I sighed. "He warned me that things go in cycles. He also said to keep at it, because sometimes people get multiple offers and things open up late in the game. Hell, I don't care if I get someone else's sloppy seconds."

"He's right. It doesn't much matter in the end. That's how I got into the program, you know."

"Really?"

"Yeah. I didn't get in on the first go 'round. Someone else dropped out and they called me the day before classes started."

"Hmmm," I said as I shifted to fold my legs under on the couch.

"So, do you respect me less?"

"Of course not, you dumb ass."

Greg gestured over to a pile of papers on my kitchen table. "Sure hope there is no application to the diplomatic corps on that pile."

"You know what I mean."

He laughed. "Yeah. Sure. So what's next? What applications are still live?"

I got up and rifled through the pile, looking for a manila folder. Finding it at the bottom of the heap, I opened it to examine a list scribbled on the inside left cover. "A postdoc at Penn, another postdoc at Johns Hopkins, a tenure track job at King's in Halifax and a postdoc in Oxford."

Greg frowned. "Nothing in Toronto?"

I shook my head. "*Nada*."

"Not even at York?"

"Nothing that wasn't sessional."

"Why are you being so picky, Lil?"

"What do you mean?"

"You're not willing to take sessional appointments? Don't you want to stay in Toronto?"

He just didn't get it. "You know what happens if you stay in the same place. You're branded an underachiever, an institutional nepotist at best and a contract lifer at worst."

"Maybe in a hot market, but not today."

"Believe me. I've had lots to time to think it over. Strategically I think it's too soon to throw in that towel. Do you know how hard it is to break out of those chains? Once a sessional, always a sessional, and then someone a couple of years younger gets the serious tenure-track posting."

He leaned towards me, balancing his chair on two legs. "You mean someone like me?"

"Yeah," I said before I realized how that came out. "No." I sighed. "I was speaking metaphorically."

He put up his hands. "Hey, don't worry. I know you're a better scholar than I am. I've hit another slump and haven't written much for a couple of months now. I didn't want to say anything. You've been filling out bullshit applications, taking contracts that pay real money, even working on articles and your book. I know you want this. Badly. But you've got to spread the risk."

I thought about what he'd said for a minute. Lately, I was quick to answer and often defensive. There wasn't any point, or any need, to be defensive with Greg. "I am spreading the risk, great oracle. I'm applying for postdocs. If I get one, that's terrific, but it still means I'll be back on the job market in a couple of years."

He perked up. "Then maybe we can land jobs at the same university. I should be done by then."

"Wouldn't that be amazing?"

"And we wouldn't have to restrict ourselves to Toronto, Lil. A fresh start in New York City, or Boston, or maybe even London."

"See, being picky is addictive, eh?"

He leaned back so that his chair was now squarely on the floor. "Yeah, I get it. But what happens if nothing comes through this cycle?"

The hard reality of his words hit me in the chest like a two-by-four. Suddenly I felt nauseous. Greg looked at me and realized he'd deflated me with nine short words. He leapt up from his chair and in a flash was sitting beside me on the couch.

"Oh, Lil, I'm sorry."

The tears welled up in my eyes and there was nothing I could do to stop them. Without missing a beat, Greg wrapped me in his arms and rocked me gently as he whispered in my ear.

"Everything will work out. It will."

"But what if ..."

"Shhhh. Don't worry. You're smart. You're diligent. And you're real easy on the eyes."

"That doesn't matter," I wailed.

"Well, it doesn't hurt."

It was getting harder to breathe and speak as I cried. "What will I do if ... ?"

"Believe! It'll happen. It has to happen." Then he stopped talking and just held me, stroking my hair with one hand. I relaxed and the tears subsided. His other hand was rubbing my back and it was only then that I remembered that I'd just thrown on a sweatshirt. No bra. Greg registered the same fact at the same time because his hand stopped moving.

Everything changed in that instant. No one had held me since Oliver. And Greg's touch was gentle. I brought my hand around to rub my itchy nose but Greg intercepted it. He took my hand, and looking directly into my eyes, he brought my fingers up to his lips and kissed them. I was shocked but I didn't pull my hand away. Silently he opened his lips and drew my fingertips into his mouth. I couldn't believe one of my best friends was suckling my fingertips and I didn't want it to stop. He paused for a minute, smiled his adorable half-smile that I'd seen hundreds of times before when he was about to crack a joke.

"It'll happen," he said. "It's right."

I registered the ambiguity of his words and wondered if the

half-smile was his way of telling me exactly where this was going on the couch. Again, after what seemed like a slow-motion minute, he made his next move, shifting closer so that he was kissing my shoulders, then my neck, then darting his tongue around my ear.

All I could do was murmur, "Greg …"

"Uh-huh," he answered, not missing a beat, even while one hand slipped under my T-shirt. I arched my back in response and his thumb and forefinger closed gently around my nipple, which was taut and tight and which, I was sure, was going to pop off with glee if things continued. God, he was good at this.

I quickened the pace out of need, out of want, out of emotional desperation. Leaning away from him, I pulled off my T-shirt and groped for his fly. He laughed and took off his shirt, then with his hands behind his head, leaned back against the pillows to watch me undo his button-fly jeans. Ever helpful and accommodating, he raised his hips so I could yank his jeans down, leaving him naked but for his briefs. It was obvious that he was having fun.

"Need any help?" he asked, gesturing to my jeans.

"Hell, no, buddy!" I said, leaping up, topless, unzipping and slipping out of my jeans and panties with one firm tug.

Greg smiled as his eyes ran along my body. "You are gorgeous."

"Less talk, more …," I said as I lay my body on top of his so that my head was just above his lap.

"Please be gentle, doctor," he teased.

I looked up at him, with one finger looped in the waistband of his briefs. "I never figured you for tighty whities."

"There's a lot you don't yet know about me."

"Hmmmm," I said as I freed his erection from the constraining underwear. "Looks pretty standard to me."

"Yeah? Well the parts may be standard issue but, be warned, some manoeuvres may surprise you." And then he quickly shifted to slip off the briefs, turned on his side and next thing I knew we were kissing, fondling and touching until I moved to sit on top of him, taking him inside me and riding him to orgasm. When it was over, I cried again.

"Are you okay, Lil? I didn't hurt you, did I?"

"No, no. You're so sweet. I think it's just leftover emotion."

He hugged me as we lay side-by-side on the couch. "I understand."

My tears stopped. "I'm sorry."

"I'm not," he said.

"I mean, I didn't mean to be such a ... such an animal."

"It's good to relinquish control now and then."

"I'm not used to being so needy," I said.

"What are friends for if you can't be there for each other?"

Suddenly the penny dropped. "Oh my God. Was this ... ?"

"What?"

"Oh, no. I didn't mean for it to be ..."

He raised one eyebrow and tilted his head. "The best night of your life?"

I spat out two words. "Pity sex."

Greg raised himself up on one elbow so he was peering down at me. "What the hell are you talking about?"

"We just had pity sex."

He laughed. "Pity it didn't happen earlier sex, maybe."

I leapt up to try to find a shirt.

"Hey, Lily," he reached out to grab my arm, but I jerked it away.

"I think it's time for you to go."

"You're booting me out?"

"Well, you've done your good deed."

"It wasn't like that."

"What are you hanging around for? You've screwed your pathetic friend. Do you expect me to give you a badge or something?"

Greg bristled. "No. Your obvious gratitude is enough." He got up, found his briefs and pulled them on, followed by his blue jeans, then shirt. When he sat down again to put on his socks and shoes, he finally looked at me. "You really don't get it, do you?"

I had managed to locate a shirt and put it on rather than stand there, naked. The shirt was long enough that it covered most bits. I didn't know what to say so I stood there, mute.

Dressed, Greg walked to the door and opened it. He turned to look at me. When I saw the anger and the hurt in his eyes it made me feel sick. He shook his head and left, gently closing the door behind him. I turned around and ran to the bedroom and sobbed. What the hell had I just done?

I woke up the next morning feeling even more depressed. It took a few minutes to realize that everything that had happened had not been a dream. In fact, when I really thought about it, I was confused. The sex had been fantastic. At the same time, the whole evening ended so badly. I checked my cell phone but no calls from Greg. We'd never fought like that before and it scared me.

I thought a shower would perk me up so I got up, tossed on my robe and walked toward the bathroom. I'd call Greg later and smooth things over. I needed him and I was patently horrible at handling discord. One day, we'd both look back at what happened, blocking out the images of moist lips, thrusting hips, and groping hands, and we'd laugh – that's what I told myself.

As I walked into the living room, the remnants of last night were strewn everywhere. Clothage, as Greg had called it – my panties, jeans, sandals, and magazines knocked off the coffee table. The place was a metaphor for my life. Damn! I'd deal with it after a shower and breakfast. Turning toward the bathroom, I glanced over toward the front door and saw envelopes strewn everywhere. I was about to chalk that mess up to last night when I looked at the clock. It was 11:25 am. I must be getting old, I thought. Sex tired me out.

But those envelopes weren't garbage. The mail had arrived. I was stepping over the pile when one envelope caught my eye. It was thicker than the usual letter. And in the top left corner were the most beautiful words ever: Wellcome Unit for the History of Medicine, University of Oxford.

Chapter 7

My life had changed in an instant. I was seriously thinking of giving up after one year of job searching. But the offer of a two-year postdoctoral fellowship at the best university in the world shifted my universe. No longer would I lounge around my messy apartment in old track pants and a frayed T-shirt. No more binging on Chunky Monkey, deluding myself that it was a complete meal with walnuts as protein, cream as calcium and chocolate instead of cigarettes or cosmopolitans. I had a future. With Oxford on my CV, doors would fly open in two years' time. The fellowship would also give me the time to revise my dissertation and get it published on someone else's dime. At last, I could raise my head proudly and feel that I was back on track for a career.

With the opened letter in my hand, my first impulse was to call Greg. I dialed his number but had to leave a message. The unadulterated glee I was feeling overwhelmed my urge to hang up until I could talk to him live. After the beep, I blurted out, "Hey! You're the first to hear. Guess who's going to Oxford? Can you believe it? Good thing I put away those knives and climbed down off that ledge, eh? Call me."

Then memories of last night came roaring back and after a second's pause, I added, "Greg. Let's talk. About last night. About Oxford. Okay?" I waited as if he were screening the call, and hung up. What a shitty conflagration of events. If only the bloody letter had arrived yesterday, there would be no awkwardness. If only something had gone right yesterday, then I wouldn't have been so desperate. If only I'd spent part of the past year getting in shape, going out more, having fun, maybe I wouldn't have needed to screw my best friend because I was so horny and so desperate to feel normal, adult, attractive, powerful, like I had my life together.

This wasn't helping, so I tossed the letter on the table and peeled off my clothes as I went toward the shower. First step, get clean, then start planning. I was confident Greg would call when he'd cooled off a bit. He was just too nice a guy and that doesn't change with one stupid fight, even after sex, and he'd had a crush on me from day one. That was surely worth something in terms of long-term friendship. Letting the water cascade down my back, rinsing out the conditioner in my hair, I felt myself relax. My organizational skills kicked in. First, formally accept the offer. Second, give notice on the apartment. Third, store, donate or sell my furniture, extra clothes and books, and book the flight. I also had to contact the department for the necessary visa. Officially, was I deemed a student or a university employee? Then I had to arrange to set up a bank account at one of the British banks.

As I dried myself off, it occurred to me that the offer should have been made via email first. With a towel wrapped around my dripping curls, I went to my computer and opened my email account. Nothing from Oxford. For a moment, my heart stopped. Was this somebody's idea of a joke? Then I remembered that having graduated, my university email account had been cancelled after six months.

That particular detail escaped my meticulous planning when I had completed my application. I opened another window on screen and tried to log onto my old account. Sure enough, my account was gone. I mentally kicked myself – I reached over to pick up the letter and noticed the date on the letter was three weeks earlier. Shit! I could have been deliriously happy already instead of depressed, horny and without my best friend in my great moment of triumph. Shitty, shit, shit. Technology and university bureaucracy were major pains in the ass.

My next thought, sitting in my office chair, was to contact Simon. I wouldn't be waking him up. I hit the Skype icon, consumed with excitement. For once, I had fantastic news to share with him, I thought, as I waited for him to answer. He was there in five rings. As usual, I could hear him before his image came up.

"What ho?" he asked.

"Don't you mean, 'Which ho?'" I was feeling positively giddy.

"Well, well. You're looking not only pleased with yourself but a bit European."

"I know you're well connected there, Simon, but how the hell did you know?"

"Know what, El?"

"That I'll be joining you, wait for it ... in Oxford."

"Will wonders never cease?"

"You're not the only one worthy of the magical spires."

"Well if you're coming to rainy and chilly Oxford this fall, I would suggest you dress warmly."

"Of course I'll dress warmly."

"Much more warmly."

"What the hell are you on about Si --," I said. It hit me. I was on Skype, buck naked. "Jesus!" I leapt up, out of view of the camera, grabbed a shirt and threw it over my head and put a pair of track pants on while Simon continued to tease me.

"If you won't be bringing any inhibitions, then you can pack more of that macaroni and cheese you love so much," he said.

Now fully clothed, I sat back down at the computer. "Christ, I'm so sorry."

"I'll send you the bill for whatever psychiatric interventions prove necessary."

"It's been a crazy twenty-four hours here."

"Obviously. Tell old Uncle Simon every juicy detail."

I shifted in my seat. "Well, I'd just about given up after thirty-odd applications, no nibbles, and another year of academic purgatory looming, which would pretty well destroy me. This morning, a letter arrives in the mail saying I got a two-year postdoc at The Wellcome Unit."

"Good on you. We'll be neighbours."

I laughed. "I can't wait."

"And what does Greg think of this latest success?"

The pause was palpable.

"Lily," Simon said, drawing out my name like he was scolding a naughty child. "Don't tell me he's behaving badly."

"Define badly."

"Weeping, wailing and generally further delaying his degree."

"Not exactly."

Simon moved so his face filled my screen. "Madam, what have you driven our dear sweet Gregory to do?"

I was not sure how tell him. He was a first-rate judge not only of character but also an exemplary reader of situations. While I was still thinking of how to start, his eyes sparkled and he clasped his hands together.

"Sweet Gilbert and Sullivan! You two shared something wickedly carnal."

I wanted to choose my words carefully. "Perhaps."

"When?"

"Last night."

"Most recently last night or for the first time?"

"Oh Simon, I'm not a virgin, you silly ass."

"Dearest Lily. I didn't mean it was anyone's first time. I meant did the two of you conjoin for the first time yesterday evening?"

"Yeah."

Simon howled. "At long last."

"Oh Simon."

"I hope that was not what you uttered when you were with Greg."

"Of course not," I said. "It was unexpected. I mean, I wasn't planning to do it. With Greg."

"What was he planning?"

"How the hell do I know?"

"Didn't you ask him?"

"There wasn't time."

He paused. "Hmmm, I didn't figure that our Gregory was the 'Slam, bam, thank you, madam' type."

"It wasn't like that. But he left. Angry."

"Oh. Why?"

I gulped. "I said some things."

"What did you say?"

"I sort of accused him of having sex with me because he felt sorry for me."

His face showed surprise. "Zounds, Lily. You are hard."

"Simon, I was depressed. He came over to cheer me up, we started talking. You know what a good listener he is. And one thing led to …"

He finished my sentence. “The inevitable delectable conclusion.”

“Exactly.”

Simon paused. I watched him run his hands through his hair a few times and couldn’t stand the silence.

“What’s taking you so long?” I blurted out. “What should I do?”

“Accept the offer, of course.”

I sighed. “Not about that, about Greg.”

Simon drew a breath in through clenched teeth. “We men are a sensitive lot. And Greg is more sensitive than most. Lily, dear, you must realize he’s been extremely fond of you for a long time.”

“Yes, I know. And I’m fond of him. Just not in that way. I mean, I’ve never thought of him as romantic material, and now I’m going to Oxford.”

“So you don’t want him to come with you?” he asked.

“Jesus, Simon. All of this shit, good and bad, has just happened. All I know right now is that I’ve got an offer from Oxford, I want to go, I no longer want to jump off the ledge of my apartment, and I’ve slept with one of my best friends. I’ve tried calling him but had to leave a message.”

Simon leaned toward his camera. “We’ve all been friends for years. You and Greg will survive this.” He paused. “Who knows? Maybe this is part of your destiny. Perhaps one day, decades from now, we’ll all be sitting around with glasses of sherry, laughing about how you two got together.” He sighed. “I must confess that I am torn between telling all at your nuptials or adhering to the tenets of social decorum and not mentioning your propensity to share intimate details with one friend, about sleeping with another friend, whilst wearing nothing but a bit of mascara.”

I decided to ignore his jibe. “How expensive are apartments there, Simon? What should I bring with me? Electrical stuff won’t work on the British system, right?"

"First of all, my dear, you will learn to speak English as it's spoken here. It's not an apartment. It's a flat or lodging."

"Great. You can be my translator."

He pursed his lips and raised an eyebrow in mock indignation. "For this I spent years at uni?"

"At what?"

"My, my, my, I shall have my work cut out for me. Don't fret, El. When you contact the administrator at the Unit, I am certain they will pass along any documents or lists or contact information that you'll need. Being a postdoctoral fellow, you're considered a *bona fide* university employee and they have subsidized lodging available not far from the Unit, certainly within the ring road."

"Ring road?"

"Everything will be taken care of, dearest. Oxford has been attracting scholars for centuries and they have the process well in hand."

I let out a long breath. "I'm glad."

"When can you take up the appointment?"

I reached over for the letter and read it again. "It says any time between June and December."

"Smashing. I'd suggest arriving at least a fortnight – that's two weeks in Canadian English – before Michaelmas term. Our first term begins in early October."

"Great. That will give me time to hand in my notice on this place and maybe I can pick up a bit of freelance work to pad my bank account."

"Oh Lily, you will be enchanted by this place. Stimulation at every turn ..."

I decided to turn tables and to tease him a bit. "Really? What are their names?"

"I beg your pardon?"

"Who is stimulating *you* at every turn?" I said, leaning in towards the camera. "Man does not live by books alone."

"How base," he said, trying not to smile. "Come over and see for yourself."

"How kinky."

"*Chacun à son gout,* my friend."

"*Oooooooo. Je pense qu'il est français.*"

"Perchance. Or perhaps I've just added a bit of herring, red herring, to the menu."

"Herring, eh? Ah-hah! A subtle Bealean clue. Is he a mysterious, sexy Finn or a tall, blond Norwegian?"

"Unlike you, flagrant hussy, I have a sense of honour. No more talk of my carnal machinations. It is such bliss to be flanked by tomes written by the likes of Newton and Halley as well as scholars who are as bright as ... well ..."

I finished his thought. "Almost as bright as you, darling."

He shrugged. "Know thyself."

"Try not to get a full-time post at Cambridge or Harvard before I arrive, Mr. Genius."

He raised one hand, palm out. "I make no promises. One cannot shackle or disguise greatness."

I laughed. "How does your head ever make it through a doorway?"

"So many have asked that very question, Lily," and we both laughed. "Enough of this banter. Write the Unit, get the ball rolling and then let me know when I should meet you at Heathrow."

"Thanks, Simon."

"And don't worry about Greg. He only wants, as I do, what's best for you. Give him a bit of time and then share your triumph with him. Clothed, I'd suggest, but that's only a suggestion."

"Screw off! Go get some more stimulation."

"I think I shall. *A bientot, mon amie*!"

And with a chuckle, our connection was broken.

I sat back in my chair, finally letting it all sink in. No more applications. No more requests for letters of recommendation. No more painfully courteous follow-up emails to those whom I asked for letters of recommendation to tell them I didn't make the short list. For at least the next two years, I had a place to be, an address that didn't scream 'screw up'. In this academic game, all that mattered was the letterhead. Nobody paid any attention to independent scholars and Oxford letterhead was the gold standard – like being promoted to VP Communications at twenty-five. I'd be a made woman in the best possible sense, and with Simon there already, I'd have an easy transition into both the logistics of maximizing my time at Oxford as well as socially. I was no wallflower, but Simon was the best possible *entré* into the stimulating crowd.

I had to reach Greg. I rang his number again, high on the chat I'd just had with Simon. This time, after four rings, he picked up.

"Greg," I couldn't wait to talk, live.

"Who else?"

I ignored the sarcasm. "Hey, how are you?"

"Fantastic. Thanks for asking."

"Greg ..."

"Lily ..."

"I'm ... I'm ... I've got something to tell you."

"You're pregnant and it's not mine."

I was blown away. "What?"

"You're ..."

"I heard you."

"So why did you ask?"

I decided to break the tension. Taking a deep breath, I started again. "Greg, I was talking to Simon just now."

"Did you tell him about last night?"

I paused for a second, thinking about which was the right answer right now. "Ummm ..."

"For Chrissake, is nothing sacred?"

"Greg, he's my friend. He's our friend."

"Yeah, we're a virtual threesome."

"Don't be such an ass."

"What grade did you give me?" he asked.

"What?"

"Did you give me a good review as a lover?"

My knuckles were turning white as I almost crushed the phone.

"Your silence speaks volumes, Lil. Sorry to have disappointed you. You know what they say, 'Once a B-minus student, always a B-minus student.'"

"You morose ass."

"You're repeating yourself."

I cut him off. "I called to share the fact that I got a position in Oxford. For two years."

"Great. If you get a job offer, you'll have the trifecta."

"A what?"

"It's a horse racing bet. Picking the first, second and third in the same race."

"I didn't know you were a racing fan."

"There's a *lot* you don't know about me, Lily."

"Apparently."

"Congrats!" he said. "You can join Simon in merry old England. Don't worry about me. I'll be here, plugging away, the third-rate scholar of our little threesome."

I could feel tears welling up, as much from anger as from frustration. "So this is how we leave it? You being all pissy. This is the best thing that's ever happened to me."

"Funny, that's what I thought last night."

"That was sex. Good sex. Great sex, even, but I didn't take a PhD just to have sex with my friends. I can't make a career out of that."

"Based on last night, you could consider ..."

I'd had enough. Hurt or not, nobody insinuated I was a whore.

"Screw you!" I said and hung up before I could hear his reply.

The next few months flew by. I did manage to pick up some on-line writing in addition to some grant editing work at the university research office to bolster my bank account. I gave my landlord notice, packed up the books and clothes I wanted to keep, gave fourteen bags of stuff to Goodwill, and packed everything I was taking to Oxford, including research notes, into just three suitcases. Simon had been right: the administrator at the Unit took care of all the details.

Greg eventually emailed. He apologized for not congratulating me and wrote that he was going off to his brother's cottage for a few months alone to avoid distractions as he pressed on with his dissertation. He didn't ask when I was going to Oxford. Typing my reply, at first I included a line with the date of my flight, but something made me re-read the message and, in the end, I deleted that line. If he was trying to concentrate on his dissertation, I'd give him the space he needed. The truth was, I couldn't face another fight. I had no idea where we might end up.

As I sat in the taxi on my way to the airport that mid-September day, it struck me that I was alone. No husband. No boyfriend. No kids. I'd imagined having both Greg and Simon in my life forever. I had pictured Greg seeing me off at the airport, helping carry my bags to the check-in desk, giving me a warm hug before I joined other travelers in the security line and waiting to be sure I was through before turning away.

My friends were scattered around the globe. Soon I would be reunited with one of them. Life was strange. I had imagined being so consumed with a bright future that my feet didn't touch the ground. As the taxi pulled up to the curb at Pearson, it felt nothing like that at all. It was far more complicated.

CHAPTER 8

THE FLIGHT WAS SMOOTH BUT THERE WAS NO DENYING THAT jetlag made me feel punch drunk. I managed to sleep, getting about three hours' rest before waking and watching a film to pass the time. Although breakfast was offered on the plane, I'd just finished dinner a few hours earlier and could only stomach a cup of tea. The plane touched down at Heathrow just after ten-thirty in the morning. I'd forgotten just how long the walk was in Terminal 3 from the Air Canada gate to customs. Like a lemming, I followed the crowd, got to the right line and was concentrating hard when queried by the customs officer. When he asked for the visa papers it took me a moment to find them in my addled state, but everything was in order so he exchanged the papers for a stamp in my passport that said I was free to enter the UK as often as I wished for the duration of my fellowship. Simon was right. The administrators knew what they were doing and everyone knew Oxford.

My next worry was alleviated when I saw my bags on the belt line. Loaded up, I passed out of the baggage hall, past the last chance Duty Free shop and out into the arrivals area. The rails that contained the arriving passengers reminded me of the chute that funnels cattle to slaughter and I wondered if that was an omen. I wrote a mental memo to self: must not drink two glasses of wine on long-haul flights. I was beginning to panic when I couldn't pick out a familiar face in the waiting crowd.

Then he turned around. Simon had been leaning against a post, reading, when he happened to glance up and see me. He looked every inch the English scholar, his lanky frame clothed in a cotton shirt, tweed blazer, and jeans with a long scarf wound jauntily around his neck. He closed his book, reached into the pocket of his jacket, and pulled out a sheet of paper which, when unfolded, read 'Halton'. He held up the sign across his chest, like so many others in the arrivals area, and smiled. I would have run to him but I was so tired I could only walk a bit faster.

"You are a sight for tired eyes," I said.

He took the bags from my hands, put them down and then grabbed me by both shoulders. "You look wretched, my dear."

"Nice English welcome, buddy."

He hugged me. "Oh Lil, if you can't hear the truth from your friends, you're doomed to a life of delusions."

"I'm not deluded. I'm exhausted."

"English lesson number one. Here we say 'knackered'."

"Knackwurst. Knackered. I don't care. I just want to go to bed."

"Mmmm. I see your libido isn't suffering jetlag."

I chuckled. "To sleep."

"Oh, I can help you with that, weary traveler. But first let's get you and your kit, that's luggage, to the coach."

"Coach?"

"Yes. There's a coach, a bus, which goes directly to Oxford. Otherwise we'd have to go into London and take the train from

Paddington Station. I don't think you'd stay upright for that journey. All we have to do is walk ten minutes, load you and your bags, and then you can lay your head on my shoulder and nap all the way to Oxford."

"Lead on," I said.

Simon deftly rearranged my bags so that he pulled them as a train. I was left with just my knapsack. I was grateful to have him there, not only to serve as my porter, but also because he knew where he was going. I'd never before been to the bus terminal at Heathrow. A jet-lagged person could be seduced by any number of options, radiating out from the underground tunnel, before the bus terminal elevators came into view. Simon slowed his gait to a pace I could keep up with and we were above ground. Luckily for me, a bus pulled in soon after we arrived and next thing I knew I was fast asleep, my head resting against the window, using Simon's rolled scarf as a pillow.

I woke up as we were pulling in to Oxford's Gloucester Green station. I'd shifted positions and noticed I'd been leaning on Simon as he read his book. With the noise of the bustling station ringing in my ears, I sat up. It took me a few seconds to orient myself. Running my hands over my face, I noticed something wet and was horrified to realize I had drooled as I slept. I looked over at Simon's jacket sleeve and, sure enough, there was a wet patch.

"Oh God, I am so sorry. I don't usually drool."

"That's what they all say. Don't worry, my dear. As you'll soon learn, nothing stays dry for long in England."

It took a second but I got his joke. "It looks like a lovely day."

"It has been sunny for the better part of a week now, but it's chillier than Toronto. When we've got you settled in, we'll pick up a scarf for you. It's a sartorial staple here."

As the bus pulled in to the bay, I took a closer look at the scarf.

"That thing must be six feet long." I ran my fingers along it. "And it's wool."

"If my neck is warm, I'm warm. And a long scarf has many uses."

"Such as?"

"You can wear it different ways," he improvised. "Or use it to bind burst luggage. Or even ..." and he quickly twisted it into a noose. "As a prop to show lecturers how boring they are!"

The bus driver turned off the engine and opened the door. As everyone filed out, they said 'Cheers' to the driver. I did the same and while waiting for the driver to open the luggage bay, asked Simon, "Why cheers?"

"We're a civilized society here, El. We acknowledge our fellow man and the service he provides. I've seen rubes get off a bus without thanking the driver chastised with a frosty, 'You're welcome.'"

"Funny phrase, that's all. Makes it sound like everyone's drinking."

"You have so much to learn, my colonial companion."

Having napped, I had a bit more energy so I convinced Simon to stop for a coffee and a pastry at one of the nearby shops before trundling all the baggage to the taxi stand. Simon helped me settle in to my room at the college on the Woodstock Road and then left me to nap for a few hours before coming back to take me to the Wellcome Unit on the Banbury Road. As we stood outside the former house, now one of the university properties, he leaned over to pull up my collar. I guess I had been shivering.

"Now, Dr. Halton, go in and do whatever administrivia you must so that tomorrow you can begin the most exciting chapter in your life to date. Ring me when you're ready to dine. I'll share my favourite haunts. Are you up for a curry this evening? My treat."

"Thanks, Simon. I love Indian food."

He bowed from the waist with great flourish. "Then Indian you shall have, *memsahib*." He paused for a moment. "By the way, Greg did text me whilst you napped."

"What did he say?"

"He asked if you had arrived safely."

"Is that all? What did you say?"

Silence.

"What, Simon?"

"I said you were tired but in my care. He wished you great success and asked me to request that you not try to contact him now. He believes it's better you concentrate on your new position here while he gives his work top priority in Toronto."

I was hurt. "Christ, I never kept him from his work."

"You, my dear, are unintentionally distracting."

I shook my head. "I'll deal with this later."

"Good tack." He grabbed me by the shoulders and pivoted me so I was facing the walkway up to the Unit building. "Now, go in and see your new office."

I was still reeling from Greg's message, but Simon spoke sense. There was nothing to be gained from trying to understand what the hell Greg was thinking, at least not from thousands of miles away. I sighed.

Simon leaned down to whisper in my ear. "This is where every serious scholar wants to be. They come from all over the world to this small town. You belong in Oxford, Lily." And then he tapped me twice on the bottom like he would a three-year-old and I dutifully obeyed.

I went up the stairs, stood on the porch facing a large wooden door and pressed the door bell. Looking over my shoulders, I saw Simon striding back toward the City Centre. For the first time, I noticed the dampness, even on a sunny afternoon. Suddenly the door opened and I was greeted by an attractive blonde woman.

"May I help you?"

"I'm Lily Halton, the new postdoctoral fellow."

Her smile was warm and genuine as she extended her hand. "Yes, Dr. Halton. Please come in. I'm Clare Carroll, the Unit Administrator. How was your flight? May I get you a cup of tea?"

I was definitely going to like it here.

Chapter 9

Oxford really was the place to be for anyone who wanted to establish a solid academic foundation. Simon and I were the only graduates from our Toronto program choosing to do postdoctoral work abroad. The fact he was now in Oxford was no surprise but I'm sure my supervisor never had me pegged for the big leagues. Strange, too, how my thoughts turned to Oliver recently. I wanted desperately to let him know I had arrived. Mercifully, I was too busy in those weeks leading up to Michaelmas Term to compose an email to him.

Clare was a wonderfully efficient administrator. She introduced me to other visiting scholars from India, Australia, Germany and the US with whom I'd be sharing the annex Unit building next door. The full-time faculty had offices in the main building, along with Clare, the Unit secretary Linda, and the library. My office was furnished with a desk, chair, and more bookshelves than I would ever need. It faced the back garden and so as soon as I got the keys, I went in and repositioned the desk to face the window so I had a view.

Simon was a wonderful help and kept me focused on my future. He introduced me to the Oxford history of science group, many of whose names I had seen on the spines of texts during my course work in Toronto. The Oxford scholarly community was vast. Once I was duly plugged into it, my days and nights were filled with possibilities for broadening my intellectual perspectives and my social circles. Over the first weeks of term, there were receptions to welcome new students and fellows, lectures, often followed by more receptions, and nights at the local gownie pubs frequented by university students.

Beyond the world of the Unit, there were also events within the wider Oxford community, including concerts at the Sheldonian, debates at college, visits to Pitt Rivers Museum or The Ashmolean Museum, performances at the Oxford Playhouse, and college sports. One night in the college pub I met a woman who played field hockey. She invited me to come out that Sunday to play. It was a much faster game than I had remembered from grade school and I felt like a lumbering slob lagging behind students ten years my junior. I far preferred Canadian hockey and so I started playing ice hockey again, this time for the Oxford Women's Ice Hockey team. They were thrilled when I told them I was Canadian because for them that meant that I could skate before I could walk. Truth was, I was only an average player. But I was a goalie and keepers were rare, so I was taken up in a flash. The commitment of my teammates impressed me. Other than four other foreigners from Norway, Sweden and the US, the English natives had never been on ice hockey skates before but were, as Simon would say, dead keen to learn. We practiced two nights a week, from ten-thirty until after midnight. Simon came to watch every one of our home matches, even though he didn't fully understand the game.

Before the hockey season started in earnest, Simon took me to Stratford-upon-Avon. He indulged my desire to decorate my room with a brass rubbing done beside the Avon River one cool afternoon before we went off to see a play. Another weekend, we went up to Blenheim Palace in nearby Woodstock, and a week later cycled to The Trout, an enchanting pub just inside the Oxford ring road. I was having the time of my life. Sitting outside at The Trout, leaning on a stone wall, watching the sun's rays bounce on the river as the resident peacock patrolled the green, I took a deep breath. I wanted to share all this with Greg, but was not eager to be rebuffed. I was optimistic that, given time, he would come around. Simon agreed.

"He's adjusting," he said, "to you and I being here and his dissertation still in progress."

"I guess."

"He won't be able to stay away for long, I predict."

"You think so?"

"Who could resist all this, and free lodging while visiting?"

I laughed. "You've got a point. I mean, spot on."

"You are a quick study, El."

I broached another sensitive topic. "Simon, what will you do next year, when your fellowship is over?"

"Ah, the Inquisition."

"No. Just a friendly question."

"Well, dearest neophyte, much depends on my publisher."

"Oh, that's right. When will your book come out?"

"My editor said this spring."

"And?"

"That should strengthen my CV."

I sipped at my cider before posing my next question. "Do you want to stay in the UK?"

Simon raised an eyebrow. "Versus returning to Toronto?"

"Yes."

"It's less about the location than the institution. I could be seduced across the pond, but I do feel that both my work and my temperament are better suited to English academic life."

I nodded. "You're definitely in your element here."

"How so?"

"You seem much less eccentric here."

"I thought Canadians had the reputation of being unflaggingly polite."

I reached across the wooden table to slap at his arm. He flinched as if mortally wounded.

"You are an ice hockey playing brute, Lily."

I laughed. "Oh, great oracle of academe, teach me how I can follow in your footsteps and get oodles of job offers from exciting places on this enchanted isle."

Simon stretched out his lanky frame and clasped his hands behind his head. "Well my friend, to be brutally honest, you might have a tough go. Not because your work is subpar or your publication list is short but because the top ranked unis here tend to hire their own. Unlike Canadian schools, which are intrigued by new blood, the best English unis have a predilection to keep it in the family, so to speak."

He must have noticed my frown. "So you mean that no matter what I do while in Oxford, it will be a long-shot for me to parlay my success into a tenure-track job here?"

Simon shook his head. "I believe that is the case."

"But you …"

"Even though I ventured to your side of the Atlantic for the doctorate, my other degrees are from Cambridge, so I'm deemed to be a familiar prospect." He raised his hand to his chest and feigned being hurt. "Makes me feel cheap and tawdry."

I could feel my ears getting red with anger. "Well, I've succeeded where others said it was impossible before."

"And I adore you for your pluck."

My reaction to his words was visceral. I balled up the napkin that sat in my lap and tossed it at Simon. He dodged the toss and it glanced off his cheek.

"I hate being called plucky."

"Duly noted. It was a compliment. You needn't take only my word on this. Ask anyone else you trust here. It will be an uphill struggle."

I sighed. "You know, buddy. I was having a fine day until you brought the whole mood down. What the hell am I doing here?"

"I'm just trying to be honest with you. You and I are likely destined for different paths, both academic, to be sure, and it will be easier for me to get a post here and easier for you in North America."

I shrugged. "Damn. I've already developed a taste for stilton and a good curry."

"No matter what happens, dearest, *mi casa e su casa*."

Disappointment dripped from my words. "Say that in Latin, you posh git!"

Simon paused for a second. "*Domus meus vestri*."

"That's a real comfort."

"Now, don't sulk, Lily. It's unbecoming and pointless. I may be wrong – rare, I know, but it is theoretically possible. So press on. Get that manuscript to your publisher, immerse yourself in your new research, and see where it takes you. In any case, there is nothing to gain from being poor company."

"Easy for you to say."

"Sparkling, convivial companion that I am!"

"Smart ass."

"Yes, smart, too," he said, grinning. He was so brash and so sure of himself that there was nothing to do but laugh.

"You're incorrigible."

"So many seem to think. Now let's get back so you can write a few more pages before this day ends."

We left The Trout and cycled back along the Banbury Road. Riding along, on a crisp and clear autumn day, I pushed any nagging doubts out of my mind to enjoy myself. Simon could always be counted on to be stellar company as well as to be straightforward and honest.

The next day, I canvassed all my colleagues at the Unit about the job market. Of the recent hires at Oxford, how many were trained abroad? By the day's end, Simon's statistics were vindicated. All but two took at least one degree at Oxford before being hired. One of the two outliers had a doctorate from Harvard and the other was a Sorbonne graduate.

Lying in bed that night, I couldn't sleep. My mind swirled with various scenarios, none of which were pretty, none of which kept me in Oxford after the fellowship. I was furious that I was still awake, working myself up with these self-defeating views of my future. This never happened when I was working in PR. How did I go from being so sure of myself, so confident, to so easily rocked?

I was wide awake now, so screw it, I told myself. I turned on the light at my small desk and opened my computer. If I was up, I'd write. That night, I finished the chapter I'd been drafting for the past two weeks. The key was to work harder and better than everyone else on the market, I thought. The rest would take care of itself.

I spent Christmas with Simon and some of his friends in Oxford. It was a veritable United Nations, his flat filled with those of us who couldn't afford to fly home or who had no family with whom to spend the holidays. Neither Simon nor I had parents anymore and my brother was too busy with his business to care about the holidays. We muddled our way through roasting a small turkey, purchased fresh at the Oxford market. I tried a recipe for potato and stilton soup. Roast potatoes, beets, shallots and carrots, cranberry sauce and mushroom gravy, and a homemade pie rounded out the menu. Simon was in charge of D&L, short for decorations and libations, so the table looked like a prop in a magazine spread and with sherry, wine and beer aplenty, we were well on our way to feeling no pain before the first course was finished.

Simon had the idea to have a Secret Santa gift exchange with a twist – every guest selected the name of a Dickens' character and purchased a present for that character. Then we went around the room selecting and poaching gifts from each other until everyone had a present. I ended up with the Miss Havisham lace teddy and knew that was the manifestation of Simon's wicked sense of humour.

I'd been thinking about Greg and wondered what he was doing for the holidays. He had family so I knew he wouldn't be alone, but I still felt a combination of guilt, sadness and curiosity. I had never been out of touch with him for more than a couple of days. While the others were demolishing a bottle of port, I slipped away to Simon's room for some privacy. Lying back on his bed, covered in coats, scarves and hats, I pulled out my mobile and dialed Greg's cell phone. It seemed like days had passed before he picked up. I could hear voices in the background.

"Hello? Lil?"

"Merry Christmas you reprobate."

"Happy solstice to you too, your poshness."

He was smiling. I could hear it in his voice. We would be fine.

"Are you at your parents?" I asked.

"Yup. Preparing to make an ass of myself, stuffing my face."

I wanted to say something cute like, "And you have such a fine ass," but thought it was too soon to get back to that type of teasing. Now that I'd seen his fine ass, it was more than a joke between friends, so I was silent.

"What about you? Did you and Simon hunt a pheasant or a stag for your dinner?"

I laughed. "No. We went to the market and picked up a turkey. A bunch of Simon's friends came over. We're all lost souls, from Canada, India, New Zealand, Australia and Norway. Everyone chipped in and we had a terrific meal. Now we're into the liquid desserts."

"Sherry and port?"

"Yup. That stuff packs a wallop. I'm sticking to cider for as long as I can."

"Careful or you'll wake up tomorrow morning, dressed as a sexy elf, with a naked quantum physicist beside you."

"An elf?"

He laughed. "That's what scares you most in that scenario, Lil?"

It was so good to connect with him. I almost blurted out, "Greg, I've missed you." Instead I changed the subject. "So, how's work going?"

He paused for a second. "Pretty well, actually. I've finished the first draft and now I'm re-reading it, cutting out all the repetitive bits and smoothing out the writing. I need to add a bunch of sources to the lit review chapter, but that's just typing."

"Great."

"Yeah, I think I might be able to submit this spring, maybe even convocate in June if the administrivia doesn't hold me up."

"That means you'll be on the postdoc or job market this fall."

He sighed. "Hard to believe, eh? I've been at this damned thing so long it will be weird to be finished."

"Weird but good."

"Better than good. Fantastic."

I decided to stick my neck out the conversation was going so well. "So, I guess my coming over here removed one distraction?"

I could hear the crackle of the line before Greg finally spoke. "Yeah, I guess. I had a bit of help."

"What? Your supervisor retiring early?"

He spoke the next words slowly. "Lil … I'm seeing someone."

As his words registered, I felt nauseous. What the hell was I supposed to say?

I leaned over on one elbow so that I wasn't laying among all the bulky winter coats and the stupid wool college scarves if I threw up.

"Lil?"

"That's terrific." I was trying to keep it light but my voice cracked. I covered the phone to take a deep breath and to clear my throat. "So you've got a muse?"

"That would make Sophia laugh."

Fuck. Her name was Sophia? I had this vision of a dark-haired beauty, slim yet with perfect C-cup breasts, whose laugh cascaded like a waterfall and whose eyes twinkled even in the dimmest candlelight. My mouth was dry, my tongue like thick felt but I had to say something. "Is she a PhD student, too?"

He laughed. "God, no. She's an engineer."

"Where did you meet her?"

"She was doing some consulting at the plant."

"Where your dad works?"

"Yup."

"But how did you … ?"

"When you left, I took on a few shifts. Just to pass the time and make some money. We met in the parking lot, chatted, and you know ..."

"Yeah, those parking lot hook-ups are really something." I slapped my forehead even before I'd uttered that last syllable.

Greg let that comment pass. "She's really something. Sharp. Funny. Driven. Maybe even a bit tightly wound but in a good way. And a great cook. She's a lot like you, except the cooking."

"Hey, none of my vegetables were burned today. And Simon and I actually did our first turkey without killing anyone but the bird."

He laughed. "Hope you took pictures."

"We did. I'll be sure to send you some."

"Thanks. It will be as if I was there, almost."

"Yeah, almost."

Suddenly I heard a woman's voice calling Greg on the other end. I thought I heard a hint of an accent but decided to play it safe. "Is that your mom? You'd better go."

"Excuse me a second," he said. I strained to hear the exchange but could only hear murmuring. He must have covered the phone or turned away from the mouthpiece. He was back in seconds. "Lil, thanks for calling. It's been ... it's been too long. I'm doing great and it sounds like Oxford suits you. Give Simon a big wet kiss from me. I miss you guys, but don't worry about me. I'll be done before you know it and we'll all be hunting for jobs in a few months."

"Yeah. I'm not looking forward to that."

"Sure you are. You'll be a shoo-in with Oxford on your CV. I'll be lucky to get contract work."

"You'll be fine, Greg."

"Thanks." An awkward pause. "Merry Christmas."

"Merry Christmas to you and tell your family I wish them all the best, too. And Sophia."

"I will. Talk soon, eh?"

"Sure."

"Stay warm. I hear it gets really cold and damp there in winter."

"I will." Then he was gone. Suddenly the noise from the other room burst into my consciousness. I felt cold now, as if Greg's mention of England's chill had the power to make me shiver. I sat on the bed for a few minutes. It amazed me how quickly men could rebound from one relationship to another. I realized that what we had only started didn't really count as a full-on relationship, but it wasn't a one-night stand either. We'd been friends for years. That should count for something. I hadn't fallen into bed with anyone right after Greg.

Just then, as if on cue, Simon popped his head in.

"Already done in, Madame Hostess?"

"Not by drink."

"Aha! The deadly tryptophans. But you seem to be the only one affected, Lily, darling. Come back and join us."

"I don't know."

Simon crept closer and whispered. "Have you been going through their pockets, looking for loose change? Having a wee Fagin fest are we? Or perhaps something more nefarious?"

"I called Greg."

"Ooooo, we must be feeling festive. A telecom tryst?"

I shot him a cool glance. "He's seeing someone."

"Man or woman?"

"A woman of course. Her name is Sophia."

"A wise woman if her moniker is any hint. That bodes well."

"She's probably a goddess."

He sat down beside me and put his arm around my shoulder. "Don't we want the best for our friends?"

"Yeah, but not so soon."

"Despite how some of us keep ourselves, we're not getting any younger, Lily."

I turned to face him. "Why do men hook up so fast? Can't they live without a woman?"

"Some of us can."

"I'm serious."

"Greg is a wonderful fellow. You know that. I know that. And now, someone else has recognized that. You chose to keep him as a friend. That will never change. If you had become a couple and it had ended badly, you risked losing him as a friend as well. He will always love you."

"Sure."

He smiled. "And who knows? If Sophia proves to be too enchanting for our poor boy, he might just hop on a plane, traverse the globe to find you, and the pair of you can live out your destiny, bickering and reconciling for years to come."

"You're a big help, Simon."

"A glass of port will help you more." He bounced off the bed to stand in front of me. "Come on, you Oxford goddess. Our guests await your presence for a rousing game of charades."

"Whoopee."

"I know how competitive you are, El. Come and use that lithe body for good, not for evil sulking."

"All right, but only because I know you won't give me a moment's peace."

He laughed. "I've already given you ten minutes' peace and look where that's got you. Come on."

He put out his hand and waited for me to take it. Charades and port did go a long way to distracting me. His friends were a lively group and we laughed and talked until after two in the morning. Many of us were too drunk to cycle home, so bodies were strewn around the flat, on cushions, the couches and the floor.

Early the next morning, I was awake before anyone else. I was on the floor, lying on a makeshift mattress. When I opened my eyes, I looked left then right, half hoping to find that one of Simon's dishy colleagues was lying curled up next to me. My cheek brushed up next to something warm and fuzzy and for a moment I thought that there was a man nestled close to me, but as my eyes cleared of their port-stained haze, I saw that it was just one of the winter coats. I was alone.

CHAPTER 10

HILARY TERM COULD NOT START SOON ENOUGH FOR ME. AS I HAD in the past when I was confronted with loss, I threw myself into my work. Even though we were still on holiday break, I went in to the office every day to finish copyediting the revised manuscript of my dissertation. My goal was to hit the ground running when my fellowship was finished. When I asked senior faculty members their advice for the tenure of my fellowship, they all agreed that the most important thing was to publish.

When it came to giving conference papers, they also suggested that time would be better spent writing. I thought this strange. Wasn't networking key? But then I realized that the only contacts I had made at conferences while still a graduate student were with other grad students. Being ambitious, I gave my first conference paper at the start of my second MA year and had branched out to national, then international, conferences as my project evolved. Breaking through the academic strata was difficult; I had fewer problems navigating the supposedly impermeable English class system. At conferences, at least in my field, unless students were introduced by their supervisors to other senior scholars, the ones doing the hiring, then students were invisible. The assistant professors, or new hires, were often too self-absorbed to give the time of day to students, even though they had been where we were only a few years before.

Decluttering my life opened up a window that had been obscured by all the tasks of the previous year. Searching for jobs, applying for postdocs, and revising my draft to submit for final acceptance had all kept me too busy to notice that I had no special person in my life. I loved being at the Unit, meeting interesting people of all ages from around the world, all doing fascinating work. And being near Simon was always a social and cultural adventure.

But I went home every night alone. Not that there weren't opportunities. I remember one night when one of Simon's friends asked me if I'd help with an Oxford Hungarian society ball. The political science students association was hosting a gala dance at the Oxford Town Hall, and visiting dignitaries were invited, black tie and ball gowns, so typical of Oxford. It seemed as though every undergraduate male had a dinner jacket and had tied his own bow tie since kindergarten. Simon said it was one of the things he liked most about Oxford – dressing up was simply *de rigeur*, neither eccentric nor showy.

I helped out behind the bar, but there were more than enough volunteers so I was spelled off a number of times. When the band started playing, I went over to the doorway of the great hall to take a look. I love dancing and found myself itching to get out on the floor, but this was not the type of event where people danced alone. Never one to be a wallflower, I went over to a lanky young man and asked if he would like to dance.

"I, I, I'm not a very good dancer," he said.

"I'm sure you're being modest."

He smiled. "It would be my pleasure," he said, taking my hand. The band was playing a waltz and I soon discovered he was a better dancer than he had implied, but his shyness meant there was silence between us as we moved across the floor. To settle his nerves I opened with, "What are you studying?"

"Engineering."

"What year are you in?"

"First year."

I could see it was going to be a challenge to put my partner at ease, but I continued the small talk to see if it might relax him a bit. This was supposed to be enjoyable.

"Where are you from?"

"Bolton. It's a town northwest of Manchester."

"I've heard of Manchester but never Bolton. But I've only been here a few months."

"Where are you from, if I may ask?" he inquired politely.

"Toronto, Canada."

He nodded. "I might have surmised you were American or Canadian, but I didn't want to offend you if I was wrong," he said, looking down.

"Yes, I've noticed that most people here think I'm from the US, then when I say I'm Canadian they are effusive in their apologies."

"Are you a doctoral student?" he asked.

"Actually a postdoctoral research fellow."

His eyebrows went straight up. This information seemed to surprise him. "Postdoctoral? So you're a Fellow?"

The irony of that phraseology made me smile. "Yes, I guess I am."

"I'm dancing with a Fellow," he murmured to himself, then realized he was voicing his thoughts out loud. "Excuse miss, Miss, I mean Doctor. My friend is over there on stage. She plays in the orchestra. Would you mind if we danced closer to the stage? She will never believe that I danced with a Fellow."

He was so innocent and so sweet that I nodded. It appeared as though the class system was alive and well in academia. I don't know if I imagined it, but the awkward undergraduate disappeared. With newfound bravado, he whirled us to the edge of the stage. He then caught the eye of his friend, and when she smiled at him, he discreetly nodded to me. I could swear he mouthed the word 'Fellow' before spinning us off into the crowd. I'd never thought of myself as the older woman but I'd also never counted on being labeled using academic taxonomy either. Oxford was a mystifying place.

When the dance ended, he walked me back to where we had met.

"Thank you so much, Doctor."

"My pleasure," I replied. As I turned to go back on duty, I glanced over my shoulder and saw the ginger-haired young man, hand jammed casually in his pocket, fielding questions from other young men who had yet to muster the courage to ask a girl to dance.

After another shift at the bar, I looked at my watch and noticed it was almost midnight. I thought I'd give it one more go on the dance floor. With an hour's more liquor in the crowd, everyone was loosening up, so I thought I might just have some brave soul come up to this old lady and have a go. I leaned against the hall doorpost and found myself tapping time to the music. The tune was a Latin number, irresistible to me. I glanced around the room, keen to find another willing victim, when I felt a tap on the shoulder. I turned.

"May I have this dance?" asked the most beautiful young man I'd seen in my life. He was tall, slim, with dark short hair and five o'clock shadow on classical features. He was also at least ten years my junior.

"Yes," I had barely uttered before I was pulled into a salsa hold that reeked of vertical sex. This boy knew what he was doing.

"Are you enjoying the ball?" he asked.

It was getting more interesting with each throbbing beat.

"Absolutely. And you?"

"It is always a pleasure to dance with someone who understands rhythm."

By God, he was smooth. I felt like I'd have to check my bra at the end of the dance lest I find it missing without my ever noticing.

"I bet you say that to all the girls," I teased.

"Are you calling me a cad?"

"Are you?"

"No, just an Oxford law student."

"Same difference."

He laughed. Even his teeth were perfect.

"You are very witty, madam."

"And you are no doubt challenging." This was fun. I loved a good sparring session.

He raised an eyebrow. "Ah, you enjoy a challenge, eh?"

"Perhaps."

"Well then …," and he pulled me even closer. At that moment, I felt something. Not emotion. Not fear. But heat. My body was touching his from the top of my breasts, down to my belly, with his legs scissored so close into mine that our thighs could have held credit cards tight between them. I also felt his erection pressing into me.

I was stunned. His arms were firm and his steps sure. This young Adonis, who danced like a dream, had picked me out of a crowd and we were dancing like no one was watching. I hadn't been this close to a man since sleeping with Greg and it felt fantastic.

"Where did you learn to dance so well?" he said, leaning into my ear.

"Back home."

"And home is where?"

"Canada. Toronto."

"My family went skiing once in Canada, but in Vancouver. It was beautiful."

"Yes. It is very nice there." It was surreal to make idle conversation when all I could think of was the imprint of his firm penis.

"And where are you from?"

"Spain. My father is a diplomat, so we traveled often. And now I am here to study law and to improve my English."

"And what do you think of Oxford?"

He smiled. "The weather is horrible but the opportunities seem endless."

"You must be meeting people from all over the world here." God, it was difficult to make lucid conversation. I sounded like an idiot.

"Yes. That is what I love about Oxford. And you?"

"I just arrived a few months ago. One of my best friends was already here."

"Ah. And is that friend studying, I mean reading the same subject?"

"Oh no. He's working in the history of physics, in a different period, too."

"And you are working on?"

"History of medicine."

"At the Wellcome Unit or in the Department of History?"

He was an unusual young man, I thought, before refining my judgment. He was an unusual man, full stop, as they would say here. He was asking questions about me instead of jawing on incessantly about himself.

"I'm a postdoctoral fellow at the Wellcome Unit."

He smiled. "A Fellow. I see. So I am dancing with an older woman *and* a scholar."

"Guilty as charged."

He leaned in so I could feel his warm, moist breath on my cheek. "Please be gentle. Use your experience and feminine wiles for good, not for evil."

I heard double entendres with every comment. I was a bad, bad, horny old postdoctoral fellow! I could hear Simon's admonishment even as I could hear him roaring with laughter.

The song ended. With the last note lingering, he dipped me slowly. That was the first time our bodies had broken contact in what seemed like an hour and I was shocked by the chill. With his hand splayed between my shoulder blades, he lifted me back upright and we stood there, for a few seconds, looking at each other. The corner of his mouth curved into a boyish smirk and then he took the hand that he had never let go of, raised it to his lips and kissed it.

"Thank you."

What the hell was I to say? "Thanks for reminding me how horny I am here in flipping freezing England?" I had to steel myself from looking down at his crotch to confirm that what I'd felt was real, so I said nothing and simply smiled. It had been the most intensely enjoyable time I'd had with another person other than bantering with Simon since I'd arrived in England.

Just then a stunning young woman came up to us. She was tiny. Even in her five-inch strappy sandals, she stood a couple of inches shorter than me. But her figure reminded me of Ursula Andress in *Dr. No* and her hair made another set of curves framing a face that exuded latent sensuality. She wore a simple gown that clung to her body like neoprene and was capped by a slit that teased and taunted when she walked. This young woman leaned in to my partner while tossing a glance my way.

"Juan, we're going to back to the College for an after-party.

Krysztof asked me to come over to let you know."

Her voice purred. She was delivering an innocuous message but the subtext said, "Who is the old hag? Come with me and I'll be sure to make it worth your while."

But my partner had manners. "Would you like to join us?" he asked me.

Laser darts shot from her Cleopatra-like eyes. Even if I was up for a little cradle snatching, there was no way she was going to let that happen. Just to be a bit of a shit and teach the sexy bitch a bit of patience, I said, "Well, that is so very kind of you, Juan." As I said his name, I mimicked her moves, leaning in to him, as it happened on his formidable dress side. I could only imagine the way it looked, two women prowling over a handsome young man. Any other fellow would have died on the spot, from either embarrassment or pride, but Juan took it all casually.

"You're more than welcome to join us. We're at Pembroke College. It's a short walk and I know everyone would be so pleased to meet a visiting Canadian Fellow."

I glanced across his chest to the other book end. I was sure I could hear the gears grinding in her elegantly coiffed head but I wasn't going anywhere but home. I was exhausted. I'd been chaste but amused and it was time to pick up my coat and hail a taxi, but not before I leaned further in to whisper in Juan's ear, "Thank you for a wonderful dance."

To his femme fatale friend, it may have looked as though I was kissing him. So be it. Winding up little Miss I-Know-I'm-Damned-Sexy was the perfect end to my evening.

"*A bientot,*" I threw over my shoulder as I left the pair standing on the dance floor. "Always leave them wanting more," I thought to myself.

CHAPTER 11

I SLEPT LIKE A ROCK, MAKING IT TO MY OFFICE ONLY BY ELEVEN-thirty the next morning. Almost immediately I sat down my phone rang. It was Simon.

"Well? Are you engaged to a wickedly handsome Hungarian diplomat, my darling?"

"What are you talking about?"

"When I unfolded my newspaper this morning, I saw no cover story about a drunken woman causing a diplomatic incident. I presume you had a perfectly banal evening."

I paused for a second. "Not really."

"Really? My curiosity has been piqued. Tell Uncle Simon every wee detail."

I looked at my watch. I had hoped to finish some edits on an article that had to be submitted by end of day. What I wanted to share with Simon would, to do it justice, take more time than I could spare right now.

"Want to go to The Royal Oak for drinks later?" I asked. "Better still, let's meet for dinner."

"Is that an invitation or a proposition?"

I laughed. "What do you think?"

"An evening in the company of Central Europeans can change a person, charm oozing out of their every pore."

"Dinner and I'll tell you all about it." I paused. "It got pretty juicy."

"I figured as much. That's why I discreetly rang you after elevenses. I didn't want to interrupt any dawn *après-amore.*"

I could tease him, too. "Let's just say your fine etiquette and sensitivity were much appreciated."

I could hear his intake of breath. "Really? You always surprise me, El."

"Your patience will be rewarded. See you tonight at six then."

"If I don't perish from ..."

"I know, sexual curiosity."

"Hmmm ... imagine what the coroner's report would say. Six it shall be." And he hung up.

I leaned across my desk, switched on the computer and waited for the boot up. Today seemed a much brighter day.

I rode a wave of energy so that by the time I was powering down my computer just before six, I had finished the draft, reviewed it twice and sent off the article to *The Journal of Public Health* electronically. Looking out the window, the weather was still good. Last night had done the unthinkable; it had banished my general malaise of the weeks since chatting with Greg and recalibrated my experience of Oxford. I had no intention of flying back to Toronto to try to come between Greg and his new girlfriend. My work was going well and I felt I had my mojo back. At least one man found me attractive enough to exhibit normal physiological responses. Pretty damn good as I approached thirty-five.

I walked with a spring in my step down Bevington Road to the Woodstock Road and then toward the City Centre another few minutes to the pub. The pub was on the main road, but once inside it felt like I was in the Cotswolds. Warm wood and flagstones accented a series of small rooms. The place was packed. It took a few minutes to find Simon. He was in one of the back rooms, seated in a banquette along a windowed wall facing the road, sipping a glass of red wine.

"Sweet temptress, cease my torture. Tell me about last night," was his opening.

I peeled off my jacket, taking out my wallet, and leaned over to give him a kiss on his forehead. "Not until I get a cider."

"If you must."

"Don't pout. It will give you wrinkles."

I doubled back to the bar, bought a pint of cider and went back to Simon who was feigning chest pains.

"You're killing me slowly, El. But then, I've had a good innings."

"You are such a drama queen, Dr. Beale."

"I shall tell Newton it was edifying standing on his shoulders." Then he collapsed his lanky frame onto the banquette.

"Get up, Sleeping Beauty."

He popped up like a Jack-in-the-Box and sat, hands folded in front of him on the table. "All right. I forgive you. Dish!"

I sighed. "Well, the evening began quite simply. Your friend assigned me to the bar, no doubt because of my advanced age."

"Your age?"

"Most of the volunteers were undergrads and I think he felt that a woman in her mid-thirties would stand a better chance of staying sober enough not to bankrupt the event by miscounting change for drinks."

"Well, he chose the right person."

"Thank you, Lord Temperance."

"Now drink your apple juice, dear," he said, grinning. "Fine. We've established you're old, you're a cheap date, and you like fruity beverages. What was so exciting that you had to wait until now to share it with me?"

"I met a man."

Simon straightened up like a meerkat.

"Now that I have your full attention, you insidious gossip."

"You wound me, madam. But not so deeply that I can't put it aside to hear the details."

"Well, to be historically accurate, I met two men."

He turned his head slightly and raised one eyebrow as he glared at me. "You are a greedy bitch."

"I commandeered the first young man for a dance. No one told me that many people go to these kinds of events in Oxford without dates. There were hordes of students, mostly male come to think of it, ringing the dance floor like some kind of 1940s college dance. I half expected some teacher to clap her hands and line everyone up, girls in one line, boys in the other and pair everyone off."

"Hordes of fine young men, you say? You must have felt like you were a hunter on the American plains, staring at a bison-filled landscape."

"Contrary to popular belief, I'm not a man-eater!"

"All right, Lily. A boy nibbler then."

I laughed. "I did see fear in the eyes of the young men as I walked over to them, to find some hapless victim who was game for a whirl around the floor."

"And?"

"The sweetest ginger-haired boy. He was all dressed up in his dinner jacket and bow tie. Tall. Slim. When I plucked him from the group, he gulped so hard I thought his Adam's apple was going to pierce his throat, but he was the consummate gentleman and we had a lovely dance."

"You should run the Lily Halton Dance School for Oxbridge Virgins."

I leaned across the table and slapped him on the arm.

"Be kind, Mr. Ego. Just because you've never been a shrinking violet. Anyway, when he found out I was a fellow with a capital letter 'F' he positively preened and manoeuvred our way so that a young lady friend of his, who was playing in the orchestra on the stage, could see that he was dancing with an older woman, no less."

"Did you feel wicked?"

I thought about it for a second as I sipped at my cider. "You know, Simon, it was so sweet. He was in awe of me as an academic and as a woman. I think that's the first time I've ever felt that."

"Charming and so? Did you spend the rest of the evening dancing with Ginger Boy?"

This time I smiled. "No. Remember, I was on duty. So after my shy young friend walked me back to his group, and after I watched him being questioned by a rather large circle of his male friends, I went back to work at the bar."

Simon leaned back, stretched out his arms, and feigned an exaggerated yawn. "So how does the second of your conquests figure in to this PG-rated tale?"

"Ah, Juan. Well after I'd completed another shift at the bar, I wandered back into the great hall, drawn by the music, which had shifted to Latin stuff. Tangos. Salsas."

"I thought this was a Hungarian showcase?"

"Oh, earlier in the evening, while the dignitaries were still there, they had the usual display of national music and dances. But closer to midnight the party seemed to shift to more of a club atmosphere. I love dancing and thought I'd go out and get another partner for a dance. I figured it'd be even easier because it was later, everyone had had more to drink, and shyness wouldn't be an issue. I was standing near the doorway, just surveying my prospects, when the most gorgeous young man I'd ever set eyes upon tapped me on the shoulder."

"How *cliché*."

"Call it what you like, but he was an Adonis and he could dance, too. He pulled me close to him like a pro. I've never been led like that before."

"Was he an undergraduate, too?"

"Yes, from Spain."

Simon wagged his finger. "Hot blooded. Be careful, Lily. Looks can kill, or at least leave you with a nasty little life-long itch as a souvenir ..."

"Thanks for the public health service announcement, Grandma!"

He raised his hands, palms up, and then mimed locking his mouth shut and tossing the key. With Simon sitting quietly, I recounted the rest of the evening. It made it a bit easier, with Simon not interjecting, to describe what happened, literally, between Juan and me on the dance floor. I knew Simon would be disappointed by the fact I hadn't actually gone back to Pembroke College with Juan and that we hadn't fucked like sweat-soaked bunnies, but I think he knew me well. I didn't want to spend the next year and a half in Oxford, bumping into Juan and his friends, with everyone knowing that we'd slept together once. I felt they might all look at me as some kind of desperate old girl who had a fling with one of the hottest guys in town. There was no chance that it would have been anything more, either. He was so much younger than me and we were worlds apart both in experience and background. But I wouldn't change that dance.

When I'd finished, Simon sighed. "Ah, to be young again."

I laughed. "What are you talking about?"

"It seems like so long ago that nothing mattered. The whole world was open to us. Nary a care in the world."

"*You* being nostalgic?" I took his almost empty glass at sniffed at the contents. "What did the barman put in this thing?"

"Obviously not enough to dull the pain."

"The pain of what?"

He shrugged. "Uncertainty."

I shook my head. "What are you talking about? You've got a fantastic gig here. After that, it's Simon's choice. Oxford. Cambridge. Yale, Princeton or Harvard."

"Brilliance helps, but it also makes it harder."

"To make friends, perhaps," I joked.

"There's more truth to that than you realize, Lil. Academia isn't necessarily a meritocracy. And being bright can help make enemies."

I took a swig of cider to empty my glass. "Simon, I don't know where this crisis of conscience has come from, but I do know that another pint and some good food will go a long way to making you feel normal. Let's go order, eh?"

"All right, Mumsie." He slid along the banquette.

"Knock off the mom jokes, Einstein, and no more absinthe or whatever downer you were really drinking. I'm the morose one of this pair when it comes to talk of our futures."

We walked over to the bar to place our orders, picked up a fresh round of drinks and, walking back to the table, bumped into Clare, the administrator at the Unit. When I introduced Simon, she smiled and said, "We've heard so much about you, Dr. Beale. May I congratulate you on your award?"

I was stunned. Simon hadn't mentioned an award. He glanced at me and then politely thanked Clare. We chatted a bit longer then Simon and I walked back to our table.

"So this is the Unit's local, eh? You must be careful not to snog with gorgeous undergrad boys here, El. You might be seen by your colleagues."

"Never mind snogging. What award? And why does my administrator know before I do?"

"I just found out yesterday. You were busy. Then today, you were so excited to share your story that I figured my news could wait. I was going to tell you over steak and stilton pie."

"So?"

"I won the prize for best article from the History of Science Society."

I raised my glass. "Congratulations. What's the prize?"

"They'll fly me out to their next meeting. I get a medal and a cheque."

"That's fantastic."

"It was a cracking brilliant article."

"Oh Simon, it's so nice to see you've retained your modesty."

"I could autograph a copy of the article if you wish, because you're such a dear, old friend."

"You can sign it, 'Love, Simon, the arrogant shit.'"

"Perhaps I shall."

We spent the next few hours dining, drinking and chatting about our research. Simon glanced at his watch.

"It's fifteen of nine, Lily. Time to go back to work."

"No wonder you're such a success. You never stop."

"If the writing's going well then let the words flow, I say."

"I've done enough today. I'll start fresh tomorrow."

We put on our jackets and were almost out the door when I

noticed I'd forgotten my scarf.

"You go on, get a bit of fresh air. I'll be right out."

Simon stepped outside, and I walked back in to pick up the scarf, which had fallen under the table. On the way back to the door, someone tapped me on the shoulder. It was Clare.

"Lily, I just wanted to ask you if you'd like to give a talk at the Unit. We have a lecture series each term and the director wanted to know if you might be part of the Trinity Term slate."

"Of course."

Clare was sitting with some other people and, being the nice person she was, she introduced me to all of them. We chatted a bit longer and just as I wondered if I should go get Simon, we were interrupted by some patrons who were obviously watching some ruckus unfolding outside. Then the door burst open and someone ran up to the barman, "We need towels. Quick! He's bleeding."

Everyone at the table leapt up to see what was going on. I went out, too. There was a small crowd gathered, mostly students. One fellow was kneeling, trying to help the injured fellow. I looked around for Simon but couldn't see him. Then, as I got closer, I saw him. He was lying motionless in a pool of blood on the pavement.

Chapter 12

As I sat in the A&E waiting room of The Radcliffe Infirmary, my mind was racing. How could this happen? In Oxford?

It took the ambulance what seemed like an eternity to get to Simon. We didn't dare move him; someone said he could have a back injury. I could do nothing more than watch that he wasn't choking on his own blood or vomit and stroke his hair, which was gradually matting with blood. I didn't want him to think he was alone.

Some medical students who were walking back to their lodging at Green College across the street ran over. They'd been walking up Woodstock Road and had seen the whole brief, violent altercation. From what they said, it was a typical Town vs. Gown beating, with three drunken louts walking back from a city centre pub bumping into Simon as he stood outside waiting for me. One of them yanked his scarf so he was bent over, then a second kneed him in the gut, dropping him to his knees. When he tried to fight back, he was kicked in the ribs, gut and stomped in the face.

The Green College students, by this time, were running toward Simon. As they got closer, they heard the yobs laughing. "Stand up," one burly bully said each time before he knocked Simon down again. The trio taunted Simon with, "Pansy, poncy faggot" and "Bloody uni toff!" the students told me. With Simon lying still, bleeding, the yobs decided that the fun was over and they ambled off, but not before one of them reached into Simon's jacket, pulled out his wallet and emptied it of cash; he flipped the wallet over his shoulder as he and his friends left, calling out, "Next round's on the bloody toff!" One of the students rang the police while the other three tried to help Simon.

I'd been in the waiting room for what seemed like days, but in fact had been only a few hours. Simon had been rushed into the operating theatre. The A&E doctors said he had multiple rib fractures, a ruptured spleen, a broken hand and he would need stitches for cuts on his face. One nasty cut had just missed his eye and they were still not sure that he hadn't suffered damage to that eye because his face had started to swell. The only good news they gave me was that although he looked wretched, most of the blood was from cuts to the face, which always look worse than they really are. The doctors were far more worried about the extent of his internal injuries.

I tried to keep calm drinking machine-made coffee but too much caffeine wires me up and that was the last thing I needed. Pity hospitals don't have machines dispensing either camomile tea or Atavan. I tried to read one of the magazines I found in the waiting room, but nothing stuck. So I started pacing, first inside then outside, but I was just in the way of all the stretchers, ambulances and walk-in patients.

Minutes dragged into hours. The strangest thing was the person I would have called in Oxford, who would have come straightaway and kept me calm, was the very person being operated on. Simon was my rock. What the hell did I know about the Oxford medical system? When we first came in to the hospital, it fell to me to give all the necessary particulars to the clerk. When they asked about next of kin, I began to sob. The woman was patient but I couldn't explain to her that I was it. I didn't know the name of Simon's latest squeeze; if the relationship was serious, he would have told me. He had many acquaintances but Greg and I were his only close friends.

I stupidly asked who would pay for his care and the clerk calmly explained the ways of the NHS. When she asked what my relationship was to him, I said, "Friend. Best friend." She smiled as she typed that on the form. In the state I was in, I interpreted her grin as a smirk, lost my cool and threw back at her, "Not a euphemistic best friend, a true best friend." The clerk had obviously heard it all before. She generously cut me a great deal of slack and silently nodded.

Patience was not my strong suit. I couldn't do anything to help but I couldn't go home, either. I was aware that some of Simon's blood had dried onto my pants and jacket. I couldn't deny what had happened, but I didn't understand. Simon himself had warned me about the Town/Gown division, but I always thought that our favourite pubs were safe areas for people like us. We weren't hanging around in the rougher areas of Abingdon or Blackbird Leys. Simon not only wouldn't but couldn't hurt a fly. Working out for him was gamboling for the bus. The only sports he played were chess and the occasional game of party charades. He said his brain belonged to science and he couldn't risk damaging it in what he called vicious games like football, rugby or cricket. He thought I was mad for voluntarily putting myself between hurtling pucks and a goalie net and often flinched as he watched me play.

I was at my wit's end. Looking at my watch, I saw it was just after one in the morning. It would be dawn in Toronto so I flipped open my mobile phone and dialed Greg. The phone rang four or five times before he picked up.

"Hello?" He sounded like I'd just woken him up.

"It's Lily."

I heard some murmuring then it sounded like Greg covered the mouthpiece to answer. The only words I could discern were "Lily. Oxford. Go back to sleep." Then he was back. "What time is it?"

"Around one here."

"Are you okay?"

"I'm fine but …," I could feel the tears welling up. It felt so good to talk to him.

"What's wrong?" Greg asked. His voice now sounded like he'd been up for hours. "Something's wrong. I can hear it in your voice."

"It's Simon."

"Oh, is he keeping you up late, rambling on about Newtonian physics?"

"No. He's in the hospital?"

"Hospital? What happened?"

I couldn't hold back anymore. The next few sentences were garbled and came out between sobs. "He was beaten up pretty badly, Greg, by three guys."

"Three to one? Shit!"

"They kicked him and punched him. He's in surgery now. They broke ribs. Ruptured his spleen. Oh Greg, he bled so much. He was unconscious when I got to him. He didn't stand a chance."

"Jeezus!"

"I don't know what to do."

Greg didn't say anything to me immediately. He whispered something at the other end and it finally dawned on me. She was there. I started to cry.

"Lil, pull yourself together. You'll give yourself a migraine."

"Damn you. I'm here alone. Simon's still on the operating table. I don't know what they're doing or how it's going. No one's told me anything in hours. But what do you care, all safe and cozy with your fucking girlfriend."

He didn't take the bait. Instead, he lowered his voice and said slowly, "Lil, I'm listening but you have to calm down."

"Our friend might die! I can't calm down."

"What do you want me to do?"

"Get your sorry ass over here."

"I'm not next door. I have to work and ..."

"He's got no one."

"That's not true. He has you."

I took a deep breath. "And who the hell do I have?"

His next reply was a long sigh.

I'd had enough. "Screw you." And I hung up.

I got up and went to the desk to ask for a Kleenex. All that crying had me stuffed up and I already felt like a wet dishrag. My stomach was churning but the thought of eating made me nauseous. The only thing I thought I might keep down was a cup of tea. Fortunately, in the land of tea, that simple need could be met. So armed with Kleenex, some change and a mission, I walked the halls until I found a vending machine that dispensed a hot cup of orange pekoe. I added some sugar to settle my stomach and went back to the waiting area.

I must have fallen asleep after the tea because the surgeon had to tap me on the shoulder to wake me.

"Excuse me. You're Dr. Beale's friend, aren't you?

For a few seconds I was confused and not sure of where I was or who he was. Then the adrenalin kicked in and it all came back to me.

"Yes. Yes. How is he?"

"He lost a considerable volume of blood."

I interrupted him. "The emergency doctor said most of the blood loss was from facial cuts that were not that serious."

The surgeon pursed his lips. "That was true. I'm referring to his internal bleeding. His spleen was ruptured. Once we'd opened him up and cleared the blood, it was obvious that we'd have to take it out. One kidney was pretty badly damaged from a boot to the back, no doubt. But we're hopeful, given time that it will heal. The good news is that none of three broken ribs punctured a lung."

"Can I see him?" I asked.

He shook his head. "He's in the recovery room now and it'll take time for him to come out of the anaesthesia. He's not going anywhere for a few weeks."

"Doctor, can I ask you ... does this sort of thing happen often here? I mean this whole Town vs. Gown thing. I've read about the tensions that can flare up at English soccer, I mean football matches, but, well, in Toronto this sort of thing is rare. Getting knifed maybe, getting shot if you're in the wrong area or hanging out with the wrong crowd. You know, the dodgy areas, especially late at night, but not usually a three-against-one thrashing just after nine in the evening because a guy is at university."

The surgeon shrugged. "I see a few of these every year. Hard to tell if race or homophobia play a role, too."

"The witnesses said the other guys were white like Simon."

He shrugged. "There's no logic to violence or intoxication."

I shook my head. I still didn't understand but that didn't matter. What I'd heard was 'Shit happens' and Simon was going to be all right, eventually.

"Go home, rest, and come back tomorrow."

I sighed. "Thank you."

"It's my job," he replied and as he walked away, he turned and added, "It's late and this area can be a bit dodgy. I'd suggest you ring for a taxi."

I nodded. Looking at my watch, it read two-thirty. I took out my mobile, called for a taxi and was in my own bed, exhausted, before the bedside clock showed three a.m.

I hadn't set an alarm, so I slept late. When I got up, I emailed Simon's colleagues to explain why he wouldn't be at the office and also sent emails to friends of his so that they could spread the word. I knew that Simon would be torn between wanting company and not wanting to be seen in a hospital gown with tubes poking into him. I wasn't keen to see him all battered and bruised either – he'd always been fit and full of piss and vinegar. But this wasn't about me, so I ate breakfast, showered, dressed and bicycled to the infirmary.

When I entered his room, I was prepared for the worst. My pessimism was not unfounded. He was in a double room but did not have a roommate. He was lying in the bed, covered from his neck down. Monitors surrounded him, making silence impossible. His face was swollen, covered in a series of small sutures and looked like Gerry Cheevers' goalie mask. One eye was swollen shut. The sight of him made me want to weep. I tiptoed over to the side of the bed and reached over to move that lock of hair, which had fallen over his patched eye. He turned his head at my touch.

"El?"

"Yes?"

"Thanks, but I can't see a bloody thing out of that eye right now anyways."

The tears that had been welling up stopped. I smiled.

"Oh Simon, I'm so sorry."

"I am, too."

"How do you feel?"

"Like I've been tossed out of a car on the M25 and run over by a steady stream of lorries."

"I spoke to the surgeon last night. He said they had to take out your spleen and you've got a bunch of broken ribs but the good news is none of them punctured your lungs."

"As long as they are generous with the morphine."

All I could do was shake my head.

"I must say, this is a blood nuisance," and he raised his hand, which had a cast on it. "What the hell am I supposed to do with this on?"

"I think they expect you to rest."

"Thank you, doctor. But this is going to seriously curtail my typing."

"Oh no, Simon. You can't type. Not right now."

"Well, if I'm to be kept in this damned place for weeks, what do you expect me to do? Read *Hello* all day? Watch *Coronation Street* or footie matches? Don't be daft, El. Tomorrow, bring me my computer."

"I don't know. I haven't spoken with anyone yet about what you can and can't do."

"Let me summarize the situation for you, my dear friend. My body fluids are the domain of others right now – both for nourishment ..." and he held up one arm showing the intravenous lines, "and for waste products." He gestured to his groin and to the side of the bed where a bag half filled with blood and urine was hanging. "My pain is being controlled, and my sartorial needs are being met with the barest of essentials. The list of things I *can* do is short and sweet. I think I can read, albeit through one eye, and I think I can type one-handed. Today I shall be obedient and complacent and rest. Tomorrow, I'd like to try to get back to my research. For that I need an accomplice and that accomplice is you, dear."

"Simon, I don't want you to strain ..."

"I will not let the bastards win. I remember being bullied in school. This is no different, except for the broken bones and lost organ. I can't let them take over my life. They're yobs. The best they can hope for is marginal employment and a few pints. To be honest, I feel sorry for them."

"You are a strange man. You're sitting here, face swollen, intubated, catheterized, and recovering from surgery and you feel sorry for them?"

"Lily, they beat up the body but I'm not beaten. They didn't hurt my mind. That's why I broke my hand. I was protecting my head, my brain. I'll admit that my face might be a tad less handsome with the scars but my brain and my teeth are intact. Thank God! You know the reputation of English dentistry." He smiled.

It was comforting to hear his wit. I wondered just how much morphine he was on to be so chipper. It wasn't going to be pretty when the nurses started to dial it back to prevent addiction. For now, at least in spirit, the old Simon was back.

"Now, would you be a dear and straighten out the things on that table? I'd like to make it easier for the staff for all the well wishers' baskets and floral arrangements when they arrive."

"How considerate," I teased.

"I'm ravenous but the nurse said no solid food and when it does arrive it will likely have a vile consistency."

"This ain't the Ritz, eh pal?"

Simon smiled. "Would you be a dear and shift my pillows upwards?"

"Sure." I reached over his head and grabbed the two thin pillows and tried to pull them up a bit. "Can you lift your head, just a bit?"

He had been so upbeat that I was unprepared for what came next. When he tried to lift his head just an inch off the pillows, he had to stifle a scream. His whole face contorted in pain. I realized no amount of morphine could entirely mask the agony of broken ribs.

"Don't. Don't. I'll manage somehow." He lay back and I ineffectively pretended to shift the pillows. I couldn't move a damned thing with his head on them. How could I have been so stupid? "There. It's over."

He couldn't speak so he nodded.

Just then a nurse came in. "Good afternoon."

"Good afternoon," I answered back. "I'm a friend of Simon's. We just tried to straighten his pillows. But the pain …"

She pursed her lips and shook her head. "That was not wise." Then she turned to Simon. "Dr. Beale?"

Having caught his breath, he could answer. "Yes."

"It is imperative that you do not try to move. Although the morphine does an excellent job controlling the pain, it can also falsely encourage you to move as if you were well. Ribs do not heal overnight." As she finished that sentence, she glared at me.

"I understand," I said.

She turned to Simon then nodded as if to say, "And you, obstreperous patient?"

He simply said, "Understood."

Then the nurse turned back to me as she reached for his chart. "He should be resting."

Subtlety was not her strong suit but she had a point. Although he had been chatty as always, he looked like a man who'd had the shit kicked out of him. He certainly was in no condition to go home, even to the dimmest observer, and I could only see his swollen face and bandaged hand. I didn't have any idea of the state of his incision or anything about his internal injuries. I was just happy to see with my own eyes that he was alive.

"Yes, I was just leaving," I said as the nurse positioned herself to take his vital signs. "Simon, I'll be back tomorrow. You rest."

"Don't forget that package," he said.

I knew he meant his computer but I couldn't see how he could type, not only physically but with Nurse Stroppy on duty.

Appropriately admonished, I left the hospital. I cycled to my office. It was hard for me to get started on my next project, but after some tea and chatting with Clare, routine kicked in and I spent a few productive hours on my computer. I had hoped that the police might ring to tell me they had arrested the trio but no such luck. I left the office earlier than usual and went home.

I was trying to relax, watching a chat show on the Beeb, when my mobile rang. Fear gripped me. Had Simon taken a turn for the worse? I was his next of kin, the first person they would ring. I picked up the phone without looking at the screen.

"Hello," I said, so tentatively it was barely audible.

"Hello?" a man's voice answered.

"Yes. Hello."

"Lil?"

"This is Lily Halton."

"Well, that's good."

It was Greg.

"Jeezus, don't scare me like that," I said.

He laughed. "Sorry. I didn't know I could scare you with a simple 'Hello.'"

"I thought it was the hospital ringing."

"I'm sorry. How is our boy?"

"He can barely move without wincing. I guess his ribs are taped but he's just supposed to lie still until they start to heal and that's tough for him. He wants me to bring his computer tomorrow so he can get back to work."

"So Simon."

"His face is a mess. One eye is swollen shut and his hand is in a cast."

Greg chuckled. "Sounds like some sort of villain. Has he asked for a monocle or a black leather eye patch yet?"

I laughed in spite of myself. "You're so bad."

"How are you holding up?"

I shrugged. "Okay, I guess. I feel so helpless."

"You could always offer to sponge bathe the old boy. That would be pretty interesting."

"I can always count on you to bring things back to the baser elements."

"I try." He paused. "Lil, I rejigged my schedule. I'm actually calling from the airport. My flight is scheduled to leave in an hour and a half."

"Where are you going?"

"I'm coming to Oxford, you silly idiot."

I was stunned. "Really?"

"Yeah, really. I switched shifts at the plant, but I can only stay until Monday."

I did a mental calculation – he'd be here for what amounted to a long weekend. "Is it worth it for three days? You'll be jetlagged most of the time."

"Just promise you won't take advantage of me, eh?"

I grimaced. "As if your lady friend would allow that."

"You're right. She probably wouldn't like that." Another pause. "Can I bunk on your couch? If it's not too weird."

I laughed. "You mean can I resist your charms and not jump your bones for three glorious days and nights while our battered friend is lying in a hospital bed?"

"Yeah."

"Sure," I said. "Or you can stay at Simon's so we don't bump into each other in the shower."

"Right. I'd forgotten that his place would be free."

It was going to be so nice to have someone to talk to, even for a few days. "Do you know how to get here? I mean from the airport? Tell me you're flying to Heathrow. It's so much easier to get to Oxford from Heathrow."

"I am. Sophia arranged everything. She's good at that sort of thing."

She's good at other things, too, I thought to myself. Hearing her name was like a bucket of ice water in my face.

"I'll see you tomorrow morning, Lil. I'll call you when I've landed. You can tell me if I should go straight to the hospital or come by your place. Okay?"

"Sure. That sounds great." I paused. "And thanks."

He laughed. "Hey, what are friends for? See you soon."

I fell back into the pillows on my couch. For the first time in thirty-six hours, I had something else to worry about other than Simon.

CHAPTER 13

I WOKE UP TO THE SOUND OF MY MOBILE PHONE RINGING.

"Lil, I'm walking toward the bus terminal. I should be in Oxford, with any luck, in an hour and a half, two hours tops."

"God, you sound chipper for a guy who's just flown all night."

"As the song says, 'Blame it on my youth.'"

"How was your flight?"

"Smooth. I slept most of the way."

"That's good."

"Any word on our boy?"

"No. And no news is good news."

"Right," he said. "So, should I meet you at the hospital?"

I glanced at my bedside clock. "Technically visiting hours will have started, but only just. Why don't you come straight here? You can have a bite to eat and a shower. I'll bring you up to speed, and then we can go to the hospital."

"Sounds great. See you soon."

I had between ninety minutes and two hours before Greg would be on my doorstep, enough time to get my head and my heart around what I could and should bring up and what should be left unsaid.

Taking a shower, I reviewed the situation. It was Friday. Greg would be in Oxford until Monday. That represented four breakfasts, three lunches, three dinners and three nights. Of course, he was coming to see Simon, but Simon was in no real shape to chat all day even if Nurse Stroppy would allow it. So it would be just Greg and me together for the better part of seventy-two hours.

The other key facts, I reminded myself, were that he had a girlfriend, I had more than twenty months left in my fellowship, and we lived more than three and one half thousand miles apart. This would also be the first time we'd really have time to talk about what happened after we'd slept together. I didn't want to jeopardize our long-term friendship by rehashing history. I was really looking forward to having someone to talk to and lean on for a few days. If I was an emotional wreck, that helped no one.

The time flew. When the doorbell rang, I leapt up from the chair where I'd been trying to read and raced to the door. I opened it to see Greg, knapsack slung over one shoulder, smiling.

"Good morning. Is this Halton's Boarding House for Wayward Canadians?" he asked.

"You goof." All the awkwardness fell away and I leaned in to hug him. He hugged me, too, and I thought maybe this would be just fine.

"Come in, come in," I said. "You must be exhausted."

"Truth be told, I did nod off on the bus."

"Are you hungry? I can make you an omelette or you can have a bowl of cereal or toast and jam."

"And the traditional 'cuppa'?"

I smiled. "Of course I'll make tea."

"Sounds tempting."

"Or do you want to have a shower first?"

"Always the gracious hostess, eh? Sure. I'd love to have a shower. And then an omelette would be terrific, if it's no trouble. I don't want to eat you out of house and home …"

"No trouble at all," I said. "Living alone, I don't eat much. It'll be nice to cook for someone. I mean, I've got enough food for two. Wait …" Everything I said made me sound like a desperate spinster. I took a deep breath and switched gears. "You can leave your bag here. I'll get you a towel and show you where the shower is."

He was kind enough to let my fluster pass. "Thanks, Lil." Glancing around, he nodded. "Looks like you've done okay. A step up from basic academic decor, eh?"

I laughed. "Yeah, only two bookcases in the living room. It's great to have an office where I can keep work separate from home."

"You look pretty settled."

"Thanks."

He paused for a second. "You look happy, too."

"Oxford is a great place and my colleagues are great. I was just getting into a groove when …"

"Yeah," he said. "Well, we can catch up on everything as soon as I've cleaned up. And then let's go and see how the old boy is terrorizing the nurses at the hospital, eh?"

"Sure." I let him get some fresh clothes and his toiletries from his knapsack and led him through the kitchen to the shower at the back of the flat.

"I put a towel out for you. Shampoo and conditioner are in the shower. Use the mat or I'll be visiting two friends in the hospital when you slip and crack open your head. And you can use my robe if you like." I swung the door so he could see it hanging on the back hook.

His hand reached out to grab the yellow and white terrycloth sleeve. “Hmmm, a handsome stranger in your bathrobe? What would your neighbours say?”

“I’m sure they’ve seen it all.”

“Oh really? You’ll have to bring me up to speed.” He winked.

“Yeah, yeah, I’m a real skank when I’m not in the library.”

“Skank or saint, thanks. Be right out.” He closed the door and I went into the kitchen to start his omelette.

As I chopped, seasoned and stirred, I thought how surreal this was. Greg and Simon were my ersatz family, the closest friends I had in the world right now. I knew that if I were in the hospital they would be there until I kicked them out, saying I could manage. If Greg needed either me or Simon, we’d go. So it did not surprise me that he had a change of heart overnight and was now showering in my flat. Getting a doctoral degree was akin to being through the wars. People bonded. Maybe it was the number of years or things we’d put on hold to get those three letters after our names. I’d spent longer in school than I had in any single relationship. It was a commitment. At times, it did seem insane, but then I wouldn’t be here in Oxford unless I’d set off down that path years ago. Simon understood. Greg understood. We had to support each other.

The sizzling eggs jolted me back to reality. I flipped them over before reaching for a couple slices of bread to toss into the toaster. Just then, Greg called out.

“Something smells delicious.”

“Brunch is served.”

He leaned against the kitchen doorframe towel-drying his hair. He had changed into a clean shirt and jeans. I couldn’t help but notice how relaxed and handsome he looked.

"I didn't realize how hungry I was until I smelled that omelette."

I gestured to the table. "It'll be like rubber if you don't eat it soon."

He saluted. "Yes ma'am." He pulled out a chair, swung a leg over and sat down.

The tea had steeped and I poured two cups.

"So, fill me in," he said as he devoured his breakfast.

I told him everything I knew from the chat with the surgeon and the previous day's visit. I also told him about Simon's computer request.

"How the hell does the guy expect to read with one eye swollen shut?"

"I don't know," I replied. "I really don't think his nurse will let him work on the computer. Besides, he can't lock it up anywhere. Someone could come in when he's sleeping and steal it and then where would he be? He was jacked up on morphine yesterday and made me promise I'd bring it, but that must have been the drug talking."

"Does the drug accentuate his posh accent?"

I laughed. "Even more posh, if that's possible. Anyway, you'll be there. He doesn't know you've come over, so you'll be a great distraction!"

"Aw Lil, a mere distraction?"

"You know what I mean. Our boy can be pretty demanding."

"I remember." He had finished the omelette and toast and was sipping his tea.

"Want anything else?"

"Nope. That hit the spot. When do you want to go?"

I looked at my watch. "We could go any time. Do you want to lie down?"

"Nah, I'll be fine. I'm showered, fed, and ready to tackle anything."

We put the dishes in the sink and set off for the hospital.

We stood silently at the nurses' station before a woman looked up from her computer. When I asked her for an update on Simon's condition, she peered over her glasses to ask who I was.

"Dr. Lily Halton," I said. I'd once been told that having a PhD and using the title came in handy in at least three instances: getting a reservation at better restaurants, doing any business at major financial institutions and being heard in hospitals. "I'm Simon's friend and his emergency contact," I added. "And this is a friend who has flown in from Canada to see him."

The woman looked both of us up and down, typed something on to the computer, and nodded. "Dr. Beale's condition worsened a tad overnight. This morning's chest x-ray indicated some fluid build-up. We're worried about pneumonia."

"How is he handling his pain?"

"He's still on a morphine drip."

"May we go in and see him?" I asked.

"Yes."

Having adhered to protocol, I led Greg to the room. I had been afraid I'd have to negotiate entry with Nurse Stroppy but she appeared to be off shift or somewhere else at that moment. I opened the door slowly, not wanting to disturb Simon if he was sleeping; I couldn't tell because his head was turned toward the window and away from us. We tiptoed in. Simon stirred. When he tilted his head toward us, Greg let out a gasp.

"Jeezus, man! You're a mess."

Simon looked much worse than he did yesterday. His facial bruises had deepened into angry hues of scarlet and deep purple. His eye was still swollen shut. The bed sheets and hospital blanket were sitting lower on his frame so that we could see his chest, bandaged to protect his ribs. A large surgical dressing, with a patch of fresh blood soaking through, was visible on the left side of his belly, just below his ribs.

"I can see your manners have improved immensely," Simon shot back in a voice that sounded tired. He smiled. "You've come all this way just to see me? Oh, Greg. You do care."

Greg walked up to the rail on one side of the bed. "Jackass. You should have just hurled a few of those hefty books you're always carrying around at them. Any one of those texts would've leveled them."

"You know I can't throw worth a damn."

"Why don't they offer courses on self-defense for nerds here? I didn't believe it when Lily called me to say you'd been in a fight."

Simon raised an eyebrow. "A fight? It was an unprovoked ambush. You know full well I'm a scholar not a pugilist."

"Yeah and where did that get you?" Greg asked.

"A guest of the NHS," Simon replied. He drew a long breath but winced. "You are a gem for traveling all this way."

"Hey, we three need to stick together, eh? When do the white coats say you'll be sprung?"

Simon shrugged. "I continue to ask, but they're not forthcoming." He looked down at his bandaged torso and arm. "Perhaps I was overly optimistic when I asked Lily to bring my computer so I could get back to my research." He looked at me with his one good eye. "You disobeyed my instruction, didn't you, Miss Nightingale?"

I grimaced. "Simon, how could I?"

Greg interjected. "Get real, Einstein. It doesn't look like you can sit up without screaming. You've only got one good eye right now and one good typing hand. Besides, you'd be writing under the influence of morphine."

"It might increase my brilliance," Simon said.

Greg and I both laughed.

"They can beat you senseless but they can't beat the conceit out of you," Greg said. "Can I get you anything? A drink or something to snack on?"

Simon gestured to the IV stand and the catheter bag. "All baser needs being met through other means for now, thank you. Enough about my pains. Let's talk about your pain, Greg." He paused. "Dissertation draft done?"

It was Greg's turn to wince. "Smooth shift."

"Never let it be said that even whilst injured I monopolize a conversation," Simon said.

I decided to interject. "Simon, go easy on him. Greg, I'm going to go to the cafeteria for a coffee. Can I get you one?"

Greg nodded.

Walking to the hospital cafeteria, I marveled at how even lying in a hospital bed, Simon managed to maintain his role as senior scholar and mentor. I knew he was probing Greg to see how far he'd progressed and to get him to set a date for his defense. Simon would cut through any excuses Greg might have, including a new romance. Simon was all about focus, knowing what he wanted, and would let nothing stand in his way. We all knew that he considered himself the greatest intellect of the group. That was patently obvious and true but Simon would admit that intelligence alone did not guarantee success. Greg could be just as stubborn and focused if he was motivated. When he slacked, it was not out of laziness but from a loss of purpose.

I got the coffees, double milk and sugar for Greg and triple milk for myself. I smiled as it struck me that you really only knew someone when you knew how they liked their coffee.

As I walked down the corridors, hearing occasional moans from patients, young and old, it hit me just how wretched Simon still looked. I was also aware that although his face would frighten small children and bandages seemed to cover half his body, those injuries were not the real worries. I hoped the doctors could get the pneumonia under control and the seeping splenectomy incision made me nervous. We lived in an age of super bugs. It was imperative that he heal quickly and finish recuperating at home where his fastidious nature would be a boon. I turned the last corner and was steps from Simon's room when I heard Greg's voice.

"She seems to be doing well."

I stopped to listen.

"Our girl is determined to get a proper post," Simon said. "She spends almost all her time either in the library or writing at her office. I do believe my work ethic is rubbing off on her."

"Anyone else rubbing off on her?"

"Funny you should ask. She did let slip that she had a brief encounter with a handsome undergraduate at a dance earlier this week but she was too much a lady to disclose the intimate details."

"Hmm ..."

"Are you inquiring out of personal interest?"

"I'm concerned."

"I didn't mean to pry regarding your motives. I only asked as her friend, Greg."

"I'm her friend, too."

"Is that all?" Simon asked, drawing out the last word like a cartoon villain.

"Hey, I tried. She didn't bite. She's focused on an academic career and she's miles away."

"I understand you've been seeking solace in other ways."

Greg laughed. "I never thought a maimed man could be so irritating. You take the cake. Allow me to cut through the bullshit. Am I seeing someone? Yes. Is she nice? Yes. Are we getting married tomorrow? No. I'm not a bloody saint. Lily balked. That's okay. I'd like to stay friends but I'm not going to wait until she's settled in some ivy-covered office for her to call and say, 'Hey Greg. I've got the job. Now I'm ready for the relationship.'"

Simon smiled. "I shall adore both of you no matter what happens but don't put me in the middle. I'm delicate. And I couldn't possibly choose between you."

Greg laughed. "Delicate, my ass. You've had the shit kicked out of you and two days later you're lecturing *me*? Now shut up or I'll pinch your IV or maybe tug on your catheter?"

"You wouldn't dare."

"Just try me."

I couldn't keep standing there, coffees growing colder. With the tone now light and the discussion shifting away from me as the subject, I walked into the room.

"The bar is open," I said, handing Greg his coffee.

"Thanks."

"Someday you're going to make some man a wonderful wife," Simon quipped, winking with his good eye.

I shot him a look. "Glad you approve."

"Although you didn't bring the computer," Simon said.

"Nurse Stroppy said you had to rest."

"I retract my prediction," he replied. "Who wants a life partner who cannot follow simple instructions?"

"Be careful where you toss those barbs. When you get out of here, you'll be in my hands," I said.

"Yeah Simon, I wouldn't want to piss her off if she's in charge of sponge bathing you," Greg added.

As if on cue, a nurse entered carrying a wash basin and towels. "I believe I heard the something about bathing."

I stood up. "Yes. We were just leaving."

"We'll be back tomorrow to check on you," Greg said. "Be gentle."

"Oh, I will," said the nurse.

"Actually, I was talking to Simon. He says he's delicate, but don't believe him," Greg teased.

I shook my head as Greg and I left the room. We were all together again. Pity it couldn't be under different circumstances. Even greater pity it was just for three days.

CHAPTER 14

WHEN WE GOT BACK TO MY PLACE, GREG LOOKED TIRED SO I SUGGESTED he lie down. I got no argument from him. While he slept on my couch, I had some time to think about what I'd overheard. At first I was offended, but he hadn't been insulting. In fact, everything he'd told Simon was factual. Then I felt connected. Even though Greg was in a new relationship, he cared enough about me and my life to ask how I was doing and, of course, flying over to check on Simon spoke volumes about his character.

The sticking point for me in all that I'd heard lurking outside Simon's room was the fact that Greg was not willing to wait until I was settled. That was the phrase that kept playing over and over again in my head. I thought, after I'd finished my PhD, that I was well on my way to being settled. My job was to be productive and to get along with everyone here in Oxford, the equivalent to making myself indispensable. This was easier in Britain than in North America because of the Research Assessment Exercise. The RAE rated all universities every five years and awarded funds based on the research outputs of all scholars. I was working on a book manuscript and had just submitted an article for possible publication. At this pace, I was on track to be the most productive postdoctoral scholar at the Unit and, I figured, with the next RAE coming up within a year, I'd prove to be a valuable asset to the university. I saw myself as settled or at least well on my way to it.

Greg woke up after an hour's nap while I was preparing dinner. He came in to the kitchen, rubbing his bloodshot eyes.

"Smells good," he said.

"Thanks. I'm making bangers and mash. And I've got an apple pie in the oven."

"I didn't know you were so domesticated, Lil."

I shrugged. "I don't have company over every day. Sleep well?"

"I didn't know I was that tired."

"It creeps up on you after an overnight flight."

"I guess," he said. He sighed. "Simon does look rough, eh? How long did those guys work him over?"

"I was chatting in the pub, but only for a few minutes. When I came out he was lying on the ground."

"I'm glad I came over, even if I can't stay long."

"I'm glad, too," I said. "I know it means a lot to Simon. I think this has sort of rocked his world. He's still weeks away from getting back to his normal life."

"Good thing you're here."

I paused a moment but I had to ask the question.

"Do you wish you were here, too?"

"What?"

"Wouldn't it be great if you were here, too? The three of us, together in one place again, like old times."

"Aw, Lil, that's a nice dream but what would I do?"

"You could finish writing up."

"And use what for money?"

I thought about it but couldn't come up with a good answer.

"And after I finished, then what?" he asked. "I hate sitting around on my ass doing nothing, you know that."

"You could get work."

"Be an illegal alien? No thanks."

Either he knew more about the system than I did or he'd thought this through a bit more than I'd given him credit. Everything was going so well that I thought I'd talk about the elephant in the room.

"Greg. I'm sorry."

"For what?"

"You know. The way I acted … after we … well, you know …"

"Aw, Lil. No worries."

"I behaved badly."

He smiled. "And I liked it, at least the first part of you being bad."

I swatted his arm. "No, I mean afterwards. I was scared."

"Uh-huh."

"And you deserved better."

"Okay." There was a long pause.

"So, are you happy now?" I asked.

"Sure."

"And Sophia. Is she nice?"

He looked me straight in the eye. "Yes. She is."

"So, you're okay?"

He paused for a second. "Yeah, I guess I am."

Case closed. He wasn't going to elaborate any more on Sophia, at least not to me. The awkward silence was killing me.

"Great," I said, changing the subject. "Want to help me set the table?"

"Sure."

That night, and the next two nights, he stayed at my flat. I was going to offer Simon's flat again, but was so happy to have company at hand that I never mentioned alternative lodging. He slept on my oversized couch, always waking before me and showering before I got up so there was never any chance of awkwardness as he walked around naked or semi-clothed. He was the model houseguest. Any fears or hopes of a romantic comedy end to his visit remained a product of my imagination.

Greg and I went to see Simon the next two days, always at the same time to maximize the time between meals and procedures. Simon was slowly getting better and his pneumonia seemed to be under control. The nurse said his incision was healing well. The swelling around his face had gone down so his eye was now visible even though his vision was still blurry, but his ribs continued to make movement painful. That was normal, the nurses explained, but it didn't make him any easier as a patient. With the morphine being dialed back, and hospital boredom setting in, he was getting harder and harder to placate with admonishments to relax. He wanted to get back to work but with no computer at hand and no research material available, he was at a loss.

Chatting with Greg took up some time, but both Simon and I knew that he was going home soon. Maybe after he left, the nurses would let me bring a few articles to the hospital for Simon to review. It would make life easier for everyone.

I thought about taking the bus back to Heathrow with Greg to see him off, but decided to stay in Oxford. I didn't know how I might react at the airport. Emotionally I was still a bit on edge and I had to keep my feelings in check.

Early Monday morning, I made sure Greg had a full English breakfast and walked him to Gloucester Green to catch the bus. We had a few minutes before the bus was due.

"Thanks, Greg. You're a peach," I said.

"It's my curse," he said.

"Don't worry about Simon and me. He's keen to get back to work so he'll have to obey the nurses and then me."

"If he gives you any stick, call me."

"Thanks."

"Enjoy your first Oxford summer. Travel a bit, eh, Lily? Europe is so close and those budget flights are so cheap. Take advantage of it while you're here."

"So you don't believe I'll get a post? Well, mister, come back in forty years. You'll find me decked out in tweed and a college scarf, riding to the office on my bicycle, an established Oxford professor."

He sighed. "If that's what you want, then I hope it happens." He took me by the shoulders and looked me straight in the eyes. "Just don't let life pass you by. A job isn't everything, Lil. Don't push everyone away until the time is right."

My breath caught in my throat. For a second all I could hear was my heart beating. Then I heard the whoosh of bus brakes. Greg was still holding me. He leaned in to kiss me. His lips were warm and soft. He lingered for a few seconds but didn't slip his tongue between my parted lips. It was a friend's, not a lover's, kiss. Then he moved back to pick up his sack.

"Take care of our boy. And don't forget to take care of yourself."

All I could say was, "You, too."

He was the final passenger to board the bus after loading his knapsack into the luggage compartment underneath. I stood motionless as the bus pulled out of the bay. Greg waved and smiled as he roared off. Without thinking, I raised my hand to my lips. They were still tingling. Seconds later, he was gone.

As I'd guessed, Simon was motivated to listen to his doctors and nurses even though he truly believed that he was brighter than all of the hospital staff. His goal was to be discharged as soon as possible. He realized that his body had to cooperate and he would have to wait for his incision to heal, get three consecutive clean chest x-rays to prove he was clear of pneumonia, and prove to the staff that his ribs had healed enough for him to function at home with a little help. That help was going to be me, so when he was discharged I made sure that he understood the rules he would have to adhere to otherwise I threatened to out him to his physician.

Simon spent three and a half weeks in hospital. His friends and colleagues came by, which helped to alleviate his boredom. I visited every day, partly out of friendship, partly out of my own loneliness. While he was there, my days were a steady cycle of research, writing, eating, sleeping and my regular visits. When he was discharged I felt a pang of sadness, not for him, but for myself. The nurses and clerks had become another group of acquaintances and I was going to miss the regular contact. I realized just how few friends I had in Oxford and Greg's words came back to me, but the fellowship was well underway and I was making the most of it. More friends, especially those that didn't get it, would only be a distraction.

I moved in with Simon for two weeks to make sure he was all right. He was as patient as I'd ever seen him, so long as I didn't keep him from his research. He did the physiotherapy. He took his medication as directed. He didn't overtax his body but his mind was more active than ever. I think he was trying to prove to himself that the beating hadn't changed his cognitive abilities. Once, just after he'd returned home, he admitted that he was scared that one of those boots might have damaged his brain if the drunken goons had given him a few more kicks.

Six months after the assault, Simon looked perfectly normal. His arm had fully recovered, there were only tiny scars from the stitches to his face, and the large scar where his spleen had been removed was as neat as could be. I knew that because I changed his dressings when he came home. The doctor explained that with no spleen, he would be more susceptible to developing infections. He shrugged that off, saying that so long as drunken yobs could restrain themselves, he'd be fine – he'd rarely been ill a day in his adult life. To placate the medical establishment, he agreed to get his flu shot each year and to hasten to the doctor if ever he felt out of sorts.

As summer turned to fall, Simon was working at full throttle. In addition to preparing for his trip to Austin, Texas, to accept his HSS prize, he had submitted a pair of articles for an edited volume and was working on a book. It seemed as though the beating jarred him into realizing that he was not invincible, at least not outside academia. Whether it was overcompensating or just being in his element, he was a fine role model for me.

I thought of Greg often. I wasn't pining or angry. We emailed back and forth a couple of times a week while Simon was still in the ward, then less often once Simon was back home. Greg was polite, as always, and we spoke of work, both his and mine, and Simon. Sadly, I did not take his advice to travel that year – I stayed in Oxford, toiling away.

When Michaelmas Term started in October, it was as if an alarm went off for me. I knew what I was doing and where I'd be for the next year, but after that was an abyss, a blank slate. In addition to continuing my research and writing, it was time to comb the world for a more permanent post. That was the thing I most hated about academia. The job cycle was basically a once-a-year hunt; if I didn't get a nibble, then it would be a whole year before I'd get another chance. Simon was working to the same timeline having been granted a year's extension to his fellowship as a consequence of his injuries. Where I was getting nervous with each passing week, he was coolly confident. If I complained too often in his presence, he'd simply put his hand where his spleen had been and wince. It was irritating but it did put things into perspective.

Simon returned in mid-November from the conference in Austin on a high. He was being courted by Harvard and Manchester, with some talk of research fellowships at both the Dibner and Max Planck Institutes. His award was yet another jewel to add to his CV. His future was gleaming.

I had just applied to another three posts, keeping track of deadlines and application materials on an Excel spreadsheet. That list looked so promising, so many options available, so many futures to contemplate. My book page proofs were on their way and I still had almost a whole year to soak up Oxford. Things looked good, so I couldn't understand why my stomach churned most nights when I lay awake in bed.

CHAPTER 15

THE SECOND YEAR OF MY FELLOWSHIP WAS SPEEDING BY. THE JOB hunt became more and more intense as we shifted from Michaelmas to Hilary and then to Trinity Term. Every day I pored over the listings on H-Net and jobs.ac.uk. Other postdoctoral fellows at the Unit and among Simon's set were in the same position so we often shared leads. I was the only historian of modern medicine, so there was no chance of bumping into each other at an interview, if or when we got that far. I had a file filled with material that I could attach to electronic applications as well as multiple hard copies of articles, references and teaching statements so that I could be as efficient as possible. I didn't want to take away too much time from my research and writing and I was more business-like than many others searching for jobs because of my previous work experience.

Simon had a pair of interviews, one at Manchester University and the other at Harvard, within a few weeks of each other. He had already met members of both departments so he would be reconnecting at the interview. That was so much better than going in cold.

One evening, sitting around at his place after dinner, I asked him,

"Which is your first choice?"

"Both are solid positions," Simon said. "Harvard has cachet but Manchester's department is growing. I'd like to stay in the UK, although full-on tenure is really a thing of the past. That's the problem with the North American system now – tenure locks the bad in as well as the good. Some academics work hard to get tenure and, once they get it, sit on their laurels, giving no regard to teaching, precisely because they can't be turfed out of their plush offices."

"So you think British academics are better than North American academics?"

"Lily dearest, the best are the best, no matter where they're based. They will always be in demand. But I do believe with the five-year renewable appointments and the RAE, that British unis keep academics honest. We have to produce otherwise we'll be jettisoned. That isn't always the case in Canada or the US."

"So why bother interviewing at Harvard?"

"Why should I deprive them of wooing me?"

"Ah, the Beale conceit."

"Call it what you will. If Harvard has a competitive offer, I shall consider it. Spread a bit of the Beale wisdom."

"Do you think it could survive?"

"What?"

"The school."

He laughed. "Of course. I'm a mere stripling, standing on the shoulders of giants."

I put my hand to my ear. "What's that?"

Simon looked at me quizzically.

"Is that the sound of modesty?" I asked.

"Oh, I beg your pardon. I thought you said mockery."

"*Touché* my friend. Really, Simon, would you go to an interview if you weren't truly interested in the job?"

"Practice never hurt anyone. Unlike you, with your industry experience, I've never had to interview a day in my life. My transcripts spoke for me. I think that now is as good a time as any to get interview experience. At the very least, it should be quite sporting. I know they want me, at least enough to fly me to America. Like every academic, I adore being asked about my research and if I treat it as if it were a strategic game, something akin to chess, then there is an intellectual challenge to the hunt for the next post."

"You are really something else."

"Of course, it's always possible that something in the offer would make it so tantalizing that I would seriously consider moving to the US. I can't imagine what that something would be, but that's the joy of discovery. It's like being invited to a cocktail party where everyone is well-read, scintillating and they're all interested in me."

"Yup. What I heard as modesty was really lightly veiled conceit," I said.

Simon shook his head. "Not at all. You'll see when you get your first interview. It's like being under the microscope cover slip but they're truly the only people who will pour over your work with such interest."

"I guess."

"Now, let me put the question to you, Dr. Halton. Which of the myriad positions for which you've applied is your first choice?"

I paused for a second. "There are so many ..."

"Choose one."

"I've applied to so many it's hard to remember the list."

"Ah. Apologies for derailing your short-term memory."

I thought for a moment. "I could see myself staying here, but there have been no postings at Oxford or Cambridge. There was one in Wales but I don't know anyone there and I'm feeling a bit old to be starting anew that far from home."

"So Canada is your first choice?"

"It's tied with New York or San Francisco," I replied.

Simon leaned forward. "Do you know anyone in New York or San Francisco?"

"No," I answered. "But I'm familiar with those cities. And they have such a vibrant cultural scene that I'm sure I'd make friends easily."

Simon winked. "Oh. Friends?" he said, drawing out the word.

"What are you apostrophizing?"

"Well, with a post in hand, you can tick the career box and move on to the next great milestone. The man."

"God, are you sure they didn't remove part of your brain instead of your spleen? Since when were you such a raving traditionalist?"

"Bite your tongue, woman. I was simply hypothesizing that your prospects for a lover were much better in a major metropolis."

"A fat lot of good that did me in Toronto."

"Tsk, tsk," he said, waving a finger at me. "You had at least two solid chances that I knew about. Dashing Sir Oliver and our mutual friend Gregory."

"Right guys, wrong time."

"Enough said."

"So the Inquisition is over?"

Simon mimed locking his lips with a key and then tossing it away. I laughed.

Walking home, I thought more about his question. Any one of the places to which I'd applied would have been fine. I'd already weeded out the no-go institutions. I agreed with Simon that having a few interviews under the belt was a valuable experience, although I didn't know what translatable skills would be useful negotiating an academic position.

Over the ensuing weeks, I found and applied for four more posts. I was becoming a bit less choosy. When I sent out my first few applications, they were all for tenure track posts. As I ventured deeper into job hunting season, I was now seriously considering contractually limited term appointments of three to five years and other postdoctoral fellowships. I told myself that there were many paths to occupational self-fulfillment.

Simon's situation was entirely different. He flew to Boston first. When he came back, he was remarkably cool about what had transpired. His self-confidence meant that he knew he'd given a stellar job talk, an inspiring lecture and generally presented the hiring committee with, as he called himself, "a cracking good candidate". Days later, he took the train to Manchester for his second interview.

If Harvard went well, Manchester was an even greater triumph. For most young scholars, Harvard would be the top choice but Simon was not inclined to follow social convention. Manchester offered the opportunity to build a department. Harvard was first-rate but Simon would be one of many leading scholars. At Manchester, Simon could raise the bar and the department's reputation worldwide. That challenge appealed to him, he said. On another level, I think that Simon felt safer, socially, in Britain, which was ironic given what had happened.

When Simon received two offers, one from each university, he carried out his due diligence, made a list weighing the positives and negatives for each, before choosing Manchester. I had a front row seat for the perfect situation – two offers on the table within twenty-fours. He deftly used the Harvard offer to negotiate a better salary and research allowance at Manchester, after which I took him out to dinner at the best Thai restaurant in Oxford to celebrate.

Raising a glass of sparkling wine, I toasted him.

"Thank you. Thank you," he said as if addressing an adoring throng. "I owe it all to ..." and he paused for dramatic effect. "The good sense of the hiring committee."

"Yeah. Right."

"All levity aside, Lily, some committees can view genius with trepidation, but a wise Chair will see that he can bask in my brilliance, even attempt to take credit for the decision to hire me. That is savvy administration."

"So glad you're keen to fit in."

"It's all about being clubbable," he said, waving his chopsticks with a flourish.

"Sometimes I'd like to club you," I said.

He slowly put down his chopsticks and, with great solemnity, moved his right hand to rest on his scar.

"Aw, knock it off, Sarah Bernhardt," I said.

"If you only knew how it hurts."

We both laughed.

"So you're set," I said between mouthfuls of pad thai.

"For the next little while."

"What do you mean? I thought this was a full-time gig?"

"It is a five-year renewable appointment. But one never knows what other opportunities might arise," Simon said.

"Really? You want to move again? Where?"

"Who knows? It's all about the intellectual challenge. Cambridge? Perhaps come back to Oxford? Or simply stay in Manchester and grow old there, writing a multi-volume set on Newtonian physics. Become to the history of science what Joseph Needham was to understanding the history of Chinese science."

"Will you still talk to me?"

"When?"

"When you're all tweedy and famous, dining at The Atheneum, a member of the Royal Society. Will there be a little blue plaque on your flat in Oxford saying, 'Dr. Simon Beale, noted historian of science, lived here, 2002 to 2005'?"

"I shall always talk to you, my dear."

I gave him a mock salute. "Oh, thank you."

"Never let it be said that I do not acknowledge, to use your vernacular, the little people."

I picked up my napkin and tossed it at him.

"Ah, to survive the slings and arrows ..."

"Or sharpened chopsticks," I said, jabbing the air. "So when does the job start?"

"They want me in Manchester early September."

The penny dropped for me. The shock must have registered on my face because Simon leaned forward, serious. "What's wrong?"

"I just realized if I don't get anything, then I'll be here for a few weeks, you'll be gone, and I'll have to go back to Toronto."

"Is Toronto so distasteful? You know people. Greg is there. And if you have to find work for a year until you get something more permanent..."

"What a come down. From Oxford to unemployed."

"Lily, aren't you getting ahead of yourself?"

I was in full rant now. "The return of the prodigal daughter? Bouncing back and forth between my old life and new life, tantalizingly close to the dream but never quite making it."

Simon tried to calm me. "Darling, you don't know what will come through. You've got how many irons in the fire?"

"I don't know anymore."

"The odds are in your favour."

"What if that's not enough this year?"

"Then next year will be your year."

"What if it isn't, Simon? What if I can only get contract positions? Scraping the bottom of the bloody barrel. That's not why I did this and that's not what two years at Oxford should get me."

"If we were characters in a 1930s film, this would be my cue to toss a glass of cold water in your face or reach across the table to slap your face, my dear."

"Thanks."

"You are such a pessimist, El."

"I'm a realist."

"Premature conjectures," he said, shaking his head.

"We'll see."

"We shall see. So let's not start the rending of garments and the singing of dirges. In any case, this is my celebratory dinner and, I don't mean to be churlish, but you are not being appropriately celebratory. Please vent your spleen to those who also have one. Don't remind me of that which I no longer have."

I laughed. "Okay, okay. You're right. We should celebrate your success."

The rest of the evening was light and amusing as only Simon could make it. I was going to miss him.

Chapter 16

The next morning I couldn't shake a feeling of impending doom. I went to the office, tried to work, but kept staring at the screen. I reviewed the Excel spreadsheet, but when I ran my eyes down the column where I'd recorded 'Date Application Sent', it only made me more depressed. Some applications were months old and getting older each day. What did I have to show for the last two years if nothing came through? A book manuscript, that was true, and two articles in the pipeline. I'd met some fantastic people but, like me, they were passing through Oxford on their way to the next position.

I thought about Greg's suggestion that I make the most of the time on 'this side of the pond' and travel. I'd done none of that. So for the first time since I'd arrived, I shut down my computer. It was just ten thirty. I needed to get away, even for a day. Conveniently, I knew there was train going in to London from the Oxford station every half hour. If I left now, I could make the 11:01.

Riding the train, I was surprised at how good it felt to skive off. Spring in this part of England was notoriously unpredictable. It rained often, and when it wasn't raining it was often grey and chilly but today, I was in luck. There were clouds in the sky, but they were thin and wispy. The sun was shining and it was warm enough that a light jacket and sweater were fine. I loved the weather, even the rain, partly because it changed so often and partly because it never got steamy and humid like it did in Toronto in the summer. As the train, half empty, raced through the countryside, I tried to memorize the verdant fields and the topography of the undulating countryside. It was such a contrast to the buzz of a college town like Oxford.

As the train pulled into Paddington Station, I decided to get on the Tube and go down to the South Bank. It was liberating not having an agenda. I thought about visiting The National Gallery or The V&A, but I didn't feel like ambling through a museum on such a nice day. I wanted to walk outside and clear my head.

In less than a half hour, I was walking along the South Bank toward the National Theatre. I loved theatre and thought I would see if, by chance, they had any returns for one of the matinees running that day. Maybe my luck had turned – I scored a ticket to an Alan Bennett comedy. It was a marvelous play, the perfect antidote to my funk, I thought, when I heard my name.

"Lily," a deep baritone voice called again.

I looked left and right among the crowd spilling out of the theatre into the courtyard. Then I saw his tall, handsome frame. It was Oliver. He walked straight over, smiling. He never looked better.

"Well, well. Will wonders never cease?" He swept me up in his arms and twirled me around as strangers smiled and tittered.

"Oliver, put me down," I laughed. "I thought you Brits were reserved and proper."

His eyes twinkled. "I've always wanted to do that. Perhaps I'm getting more demonstrative in my old age."

"You're far from old."

"Comments like that will get you dinner, my dear."

I clutched my stomach. "Be careful what you promise. I'm starving. I haven't eaten since I left Oxford."

He grabbed me by the shoulders, gently, and gave me the once over. "You do look a tad gaunt, but your green eyes still sparkle."

"Ever the charmer."

"What are you doing here, Lily?"

"In London?"

"Well, I meant on the South Bank at tea time, but yes, in London. I thought you were on fellowship in the city of spires."

"I am. I just thought it would be good to get out of the office, get some vitamin D the natural way, and see some of this lovely country."

Oliver chuckled. "Older and wiser, eh, dearest? You made the right choice. You're obviously glowing or perhaps," he said, glancing around, "there is a man involved. Are you waiting for someone? I don't wish to cause you any grief."

"You're sweet. No. No man."

"Really?" He drew out the word as if he was truly surprised.

I frowned. "What's that supposed to mean?"

"My fellow Englishmen can be obtuse but I can't believe you haven't been swept off your feet by some devilishly erudite chap."

I smiled. "I thought I had been. Moments ago."

"Now who is the charmer? Well, if you're free and famished, why don't I make good on my offer? Would you have dinner with me, Dr. Halton?"

"Music to my ears."

"You must tell me everything you've been up to since we last spoke."

"And you'll tell me why you're in London?"

"Absolutely. There's a lovely restaurant at the top of the Tate Modern, just a short walk from here, if you can keep from fainting," he said. He slipped his arm around my waist. "I shall catch you if you do."

We walked off toward the gallery. I felt his palm warm in the small of my back. It was like old times. No, better than old times. First Bennett, then finding Oliver? I was two for two. This was my lucky day. Surely, I would get home and find an email telling me I had an interview, but for now, the job search could wait. Taking Greg's advice, I was slowly learning not to put everything on hold.

Dinner was fantastic. I'm not such a foodie that I hyperbolize about dining. It was the entire experience – the food, which was delicious, the chance meeting with Oliver, the way that going out for a meal with a fascinating man in a vibrant city was so normal for many yet so rare for me these days. I didn't realize until I was sitting at a table for two, overlooking the Thames with my former lover, just how much I'd walled myself off these past few years. I missed this. I was not a hermit by nature. I simply felt I had to focus to make up for lost time.

Oliver explained to me that he was on secondment to the London office and he would be here for at least another six months. He was alone and spent much of his leisure time going to concerts, the theatre, and watching cricket. I detected a bit of melancholy when he spoke of his time in his home city and when I asked him if he was glad to be back, his reply was ambiguous.

"London is a wonderful city. It throbs with life," he said. "For the first month, I was busy almost every night, catching up with old friends, going to galleries and concerts. But the past few weeks have been, dare I say, rather lonely. Secondments are exciting but you don't set down roots or risk building relationships because there will come a time when you must move on. I've been down that road before and let's just say that people can be hurt."

"What about your friends?"

"They live here. They were thrilled to get together, but they know I'm here for maybe a year at most. They have their families, their homes, their lives. My home is Toronto."

"I see."

"What about you, Lily? Where in the world are you going next?"

"I don't know yet."

"When does your fellowship end?"

"Technically, October."

"Any chance of getting a post in Oxford?"

"They prefer to hire Oxbridge types."

He shrugged. "Pity."

I laughed. "You sound so quintessentially British."

"Well, coming back to Toronto wouldn't be so bad, would it?"

"With a job, no. Without one, I'd feel a bit of a failure."

He sighed. "Still so judgmental of yourself. You're hardly a ne'er-do-well. A brilliant communicator, with a doctorate who has just returned from two years in Oxford." He raised his glass. "You've much to offer. You just don't see it yet. Here's to your future successes, there will be many, I'm sure."

My ego had been resuscitated. A few hours in the company of someone who knew my work, who worked outside academia, and I was beginning to reclaim my self-worth. It felt good. So did the wine. Oliver made me realize that I was doing all I could to secure my future but that if nothing materialized I always had a dormant career that I could awaken.

We were so engrossed in conversation, dessert, and more wine, that we didn't notice that we were the last patrons in the restaurant. When we left, we walked along the bank toward Waterloo Station. The moon was out and the light danced on the surface of the river. A talented busker played a tenor saxophone on the bridge above. The pathway was filled with people, some having come out of the theatres and cinemas at the BFI. A little drunk, I tripped and would have taken a nasty tumble but Oliver caught me. Steadying me in his arms, I noticed how wonderful his smile looked. Surely I'd noticed that before? When he lowered his head to kiss me, I melted. Was it the wine? His kiss? My loneliness?

I didn't make it home that night. I woke up the next morning, spooning naked beside him in his gorgeous flat.

CHAPTER 17

THE NEXT FEW WEEKS WERE THE BEST SINCE I'D ARRIVED IN Oxford. I was no further ahead on the job front, but I had the major distractions of days spent writing articles and helping Simon get ready to move to Manchester, and weekends spent in London being wined, dined and bedded by Oliver. I realized that my future was as uncertain as before but that was largely beyond my control. I couldn't make someone hire me. My present was, however, exponentially better than it had been.

Oliver was, as always, exceedingly generous. He could afford to be. He was living in a company flat in Mayfair and with no one to support but himself it was first-class all the way. We had tickets to any show at The National Theatre or in the West End that we fancied. Dinners at The Ritz and The Dorchester, shopping at Harrod's, weekend breaks in Paris, Rome, Vienna and Prague. I was seeing more of Europe in the last months of my stay than I'd seen during the rest of my fellowship.

I alleviated any guilt about taking weekends off because I'd worked most other weekends before reconnecting with Oliver. All school work and no play had made me one dull girl. No sex hadn't helped matters. I felt normal again.

The one thing that he never mentioned was the long-term future. We had a sort of unspoken agreement that we would deal with life after my fellowship and after his secondment only when that became a reality.

I brought Oliver to Simon's going-away party. Despite his attitude toward taking a PhD himself, he fit in perfectly well among the group. Simon's flat was filled with his friends and acquaintances and the wine and wit flowed until the wee hours of the morning. I spent two days helping Simon pack but it was easy because he was so meticulous and had already prepared lists and appropriate packing materials. We probably spent more time chatting and laughing than packing. There was a sense of calm about this new chapter in his life. It was a natural progression.

When the day came to see Simon off, I have to say that knowing I would be off, hours later, with Oliver for another weekend away was a godsend. Simon had sent all his books, clothes and furniture ahead the day before and had only himself and his computer to take on the train. They had offered to fly him to Manchester but, like me, he loved traveling by rail.

As we sat in Oxford station having cappuccinos, I marveled at how quickly two years had passed.

"I still can't believe it."

"That you're having regular orgasms again?"

"No, you ass, that we're saying goodbye again. That it's been two years."

"You're getting old, El."

"And you're not?"

"It is all about attitude."

"I see, oh wise one."

He smiled. "I'll admit it. I can't believe we've come to this pretty pass."

"Manchester ..."

"Don't say it like it was Timbuktu. It is a mere three hours north."

"From here, yes. But from Toronto?"

"There's always Skype."

"That's not the same, Simon."

"Then ring me. Any time."

"Ah. Sure. To kvetch."

"Whatever you need, darling, any time. I owe you."

"Simon, don't say that. You've helped me. I helped you. That's what friends are for."

"You're not going to break into song are you?"

I paused a moment, just to tease him. "No, and I didn't make you a mixed tape either. I'm just going to miss talking to you. Meeting at the pub. Your themed holiday dinners. Your wacky friends."

"They've all moved on, too. It's the nature of this life. But the good news, Lily, is that we all have a worldwide network. When you're in Manchester, stay with me."

"And if you visit Toronto, you'll stay with me."

He raised an eyebrow. "Won't you have to ask Sir Oliver?"

"What are you talking about?"

"Men rarely welcome their lovers' male friends."

"I'm not living with him."

"He hasn't asked you ... yet."

I shook my head. "We're just enjoying each other's company right now."

"Isn't that code for shagging each other's brains out?"

"Oh, Simon. I never pegged you as such a cynic."

"That's not cynicism. I was being an optimist, thinking you two might settle down."

"How banal."

"You do seem to get along, both in and out of bed."

"We do. He's smart, generous, successful, sexy."

"What more could a girl ask for?"

I shrugged. "I didn't plan on this."

"True, but it happened. So why not see where it goes?"

"I thought that was what I was doing."

"Good, but don't discount the fact that you may want to continue the relationship after the fellowship and after his time in London comes to an end."

"You know what? I was having a great time until you brought up the future."

"Lily darling, I know you. You'll start to fret the minute I'm gone and as the deadline on your work visa looms larger and larger. Keep on the job hunt, because maybe, just maybe, your man hunt might be over."

"I can't believe you're saying this. You sound like an old woman."

"You may not believe this, but I do believe that being alone is not natural."

I was shocked. This was the first time Simon had ever mentioned anything about partnering up. I knew he had lovers but they were fleeting, maybe even hook-ups. We never talked about his sexual life. I don't know why. Maybe because I wasn't gay or a guy and I didn't want to jeopardize our friendship by prying, but right here, right now, he brought it up and I was eager to understand.

"This is a glimpse into another side of Dr. Beale."

He shrugged. "I don't know if train stations contribute to melancholy or perhaps I'm becoming sentimental with age."

"Are you lonely, Simon?"

"With friends like you how could I be lonely?"

I looked him straight in the eye. "Stop backpedaling on that rhetorical unicycle. You know what I mean."

"Do I want ... ?"

"A partner. A mate. A long-term lover."

"Pity the Inquisition isn't in operation anymore, madam."

He was pulling back so I took another tack. "We've never spoken about what you do for ... companionship."

"Are you asking now?"

"Only out of concern for you. Because you're going away and these kinds of conversations are not really Skype-type chats."

"I'm not asexual. Like you, my dear, I've been focused on getting settled professionally. Of course, I haven't lived like a monk. You've been more chaste than me over the past few years and I don't know whether to pity or admire you," he said, smiling. "But since I signed the contract, my thoughts have turned to what's next. I've got my career and, to be honest, I find myself fretting about being alone for the rest of my life. Being old, decrepit, reading in a creaking rocker, tripping over papers that litter my flat, breaking a hip and lying there until the neighbour notices my rotting corpse or her wretched cats sniff me out."

"What have you been drinking?"

"Permit me the hyperbole. Truthfully, without you, I am sure I would have come to this conclusion earlier." He glanced at his watch. "In less than five minutes, my train will pull into the station, we'll say goodbye again, and I shall be off on another adventure. I'll be thirty soon, *sans* spleen, witty, gay and, yes, wanting someone in my life."

"I'm sure Manchester will be filled with countless possibilities."

"Hook-ups? I've had those. They're like Chinese food. They fill you up but soon you're hungry again."

I shook my head in disbelief. "So you – a brilliant, handsome, gay man-about-town – wants the same things as most women."

"It seems so."

I chuckled. "If I'd known that sitting in train stations would open you up I would have done so years ago."

"You Machiavellian ..."

I leaned over and took his hands in mine. "No. I adore you. I want the best for you. I had no idea that the best job wasn't enough."

"A revelation. I am ... human!"

We both laughed.

"I had my suspicions," I said.

"Did you?"

"Yes."

"You and I have more in common than you thought," he said.

"I guess we do."

He raised one eyebrow. "Pity Oliver isn't ..."

"Gay?"

"He is, as you said, intelligent, handsome and sexy."

"Back off, Simon."

"Oooooo, a little competition sharpens the focus, doesn't it?"

I paused for a moment. "I guess it does."

Just then, the arrival of the direct train to Manchester Piccadilly came over the station loudspeaker. This was it.

"Where did the time go?" I was starting to tear up.

He stood up to clear the table and gather up his jacket and computer case. "It's not like I'm off to war. It's just Manchester."

"I know but it's the end of an era."

"I shall call you from the train. If you and your lover are otherwise engaged, I shall understand if you can't pick up. But ring me, soon and often."

"Of course I will. And go easy on them at Manchester. You are quite the force to be reckoned with, Simon."

"'Tis my curse."

I winked at him. "And I bet you'll find a friend on the train."

He smirked. "Did that once. Deliciously wicked."

"Sometimes I don't think I know anything at all about you," I said.

"It's always nice to leave a wee bit of mystery."

The train pulled in to the station. I hugged him tight. "Thanks, Simon. For everything, and take care of yourself."

"You've stolen all my lines. Lily, you're one hell of a scholar, a stellar friend, and a stunning woman. Pity I'm not your kind of man," and he shrugged before gathering up his things.

"You're just being nice. We'd kill each other if we were together."

"It would be an unforgettable if brief encounter, my dear. The tabloids would love it! And you would get that fame you so desperately but secretly crave. Me, I prefer reverence and ignominy. Posterity will reward me as it does most brilliance."

"You'll miss your train, you verbose pedant."

He turned on one heel and with five strides was through the gate, bounding across the platform and on to the train. I moved to the gate to get a better view and stood there as the train pulled out. Simon dropped his bag and jacket at his seat and then came back to the doorway, clutching the hand rail with one hand, the other waving to me like a character in a black and white 1940s film. Anyone watching might have thought we were lovers saying goodbye. My lover was on his way to pick me up for a weekend in the country. I had to pack, so when the last sign of Simon vanished – his train time clicked off the board above the gates to be replaced by the next train for that platform – I set off for the Unit to pick up my bicycle and ride back to my flat.

Chapter 18

Riding home on a sunny day, I was thrilled that I had plans. It would have been too depressing to go home and not to have Simon nearby when I wanted to take a break for an éclair from the *patisserie* on Little Clarendon or go for a stroll through the university parks.

I made great time and was ready when Oliver drove up in the cutest MG with the top down. He was dressed in a cream-coloured linen shirt open at the neck, a lightweight glen check sport coat, khaki pants perfectly creased, and brown Italian loafers freshly polished. His clothes, his manners, the car: he had a way of making me feel as though I was in a sixties spy movie. I had shared that thought with him when we were last in London so I knew he was playing up to my image of him. I was halfway out the door, overnight bag in my hand when, with a giggle, I snatched a chiffon scarf off the hook on the back of my door.

Oliver took my bag with one hand and wrapped his other arm around my waist, pulling me to him to kiss me. He was a fantastic kisser. I couldn't pinpoint what it was about his technique, but time melted when his lips touched mine. When he finally pulled away to place my leather bag in the back seat, I was on the verge of asking him to scupper the plans and to come up to my room. But then reason returned. We'd likely be in a bed somewhere in the Cotswolds within the hour. I could wait.

"You look lovely," he said as he came back to hold open the car door.

"Aren't you the gentleman?"

He leaned over to nip at my ear. "For now, madam, for now."

I sat down and slid across the seat, still holding my scarf. He walked around to the right side and slipped behind the wheel. "Ready for a deliciously dirty weekend?"

I swung the scarf around my face, flicking one end behind me just for effect and then, with my index finger, tapped my sunglasses, which I had taken to wearing all the time as a hairband, down onto my nose.

He laughed. "What's this?"

"You make me feel like Brigitte Bardot. *C'est ça!*"

"Ooh-la-la. *Vive la France!*"

"Take me away."

"With pleasure. But first ..." He reached into the glove compartment to retrieve a CD and popped it into the slit. Suddenly Petula Clark was singing 'Downtown'.

I smiled.

"I thought it was appropriate for our sixties theme."

"It's absolutely groovy. It's like you're a secret agent."

"Agent O at your service, madam." He winked.

I threw my head back and laughed.

"And you say you make your living in PR?"

"It works, most of the time." He put the key in the ignition, revved the engine once, and we were off. This was infinitely better than sitting around Oxford, moping.

Oliver drove the MG, keeping one hand on the gear shift when needed, otherwise his hand caressed my leg. With the retro soundtrack playing in the background, he turned to me to ask, "Simon get away all right?"

"Yes."

"He seemed quite chuffed to be going to Manchester."

"He is. It sounds like the perfect position for him."

"After Oxford, some might see it as a letdown."

"I know, I wondered about that, too. But he says the position and the level of research support are better than anything else out there right now. He can set up his own institute over the next few years."

"That is impressive," Oliver said.

"He was also unusually forthcoming about being a bit lonely."

"Really?"

I loved the way he listened. I reached up to run my fingers through his hair at the base of his neck. "He just confessed in the train station that he'd spent so much time strategizing about his career that only now he'd noticed that he didn't have any special person in his life."

"Hmmm, that's interesting."

"What do you mean?"

"Simon never struck me as the type. Charming? Yes. A *bon vivant* surrounded by interesting people? Yes. Perhaps even sexually voracious. But 'settled Simon'? Who knew?"

"I put it down to the power of impending rail travel."

Oliver took his eyes from the road for a moment. "Or perhaps it struck him just how much he'll miss you."

"You're sweet."

"You have been his most constant companion, albeit in a

relationship that's been free of sexual complications, for the past six, seven years. You've been closer than many married couples. It's only natural that as he embarks upon the next phase of his life he reflects on what he's leaving behind as well as what he is moving towards."

"I'd never thought along those lines."

"Darling, I don't think you understand what you mean to the men in your life, straight or gay, lovers or friends."

I laughed. "Yup. That covers it."

"So, don't panic if Simon was a tad melancholy. It shows he's human as well as a brilliant academic. That is all too rare. And don't fret. He'll find someone in Manchester. He's not a recluse. In the meanwhile, you'll just have to distract yourself with this lusty old gent." He raised one eyebrow. "All right?"

"More than all right."

"Good, because I don't need a zimmer frame yet or any pharmaceutical assistance. And we'll be there in less than an hour."

"Where are we going?"

"The Cotswolds."

"Yes, but where specifically?"

"Oh, a charming little village I know. We used to go there when I was a boy, to get away from the buzz of the city. I'm sure you'll be pleased."

"You treat me so well."

"You deserve it, Lily."

I didn't want the weekend to end. Oliver drove south, through Abingdon toward Newbury but turned west just past Chiveley. Making good time on the motorway, we passed Swindon and crossed the River Avon, then turned south toward Chippenham. After about twenty minutes, we turned onto a smaller road, passing a racing circuit then turning into the most beautiful village I'd ever seen. Oliver drove slowly through the centre, past a lovely church and quaint shops, to the northern edge, where an imposing stone manor house stood. He pulled the car to a stop in the parking lot and turned to me.

"Welcome to Castle Combe, Lily. I hope you find it to be as charming as I did when I first came here."

"It's beautiful."

He laughed. "You haven't seen much of it yet."

"Show me."

He took my face in his hands and before he kissed me said, "I will show you many things, my darling. And I know exactly what I want to show you next."

Entering the lobby of the hotel, I was in heaven. We checked in and were offered a suite in the main building or one of the adjacent mews cottages. Oliver looked at me and I chose the cottage. Within minutes we were languorously peeling each other's clothes off precisely so Oliver could show me yet another way to think of England.

The weekend was idyllic. We divided our time between first-rate cuisine, village explorations, and making love in the four-poster bed. Although we discussed many things, neither of us brought up the subject of my career.

Oliver was a wonderful companion, both in and out of bed. He was as relaxed in this tiny Wiltshire hamlet as he was at the opera or a cocktail party in London. Walking around the village, visiting the small medieval church, St. Andrews, he wanted to show me the tomb of Sir Walter de Dunstanville, a Norman knight who took part in two crusades. The flowers in the church were beautiful and he told me that this small church was known for the stunning arrangements, all created by the local residents. He managed to inform without lecturing and to listen without losing focus. It struck me that perhaps this was a reflection of both self-confidence and age – younger men were either always trying to impress with endless chatter or listening only to appear sensitive as a prelude to getting a woman into bed.

All too quickly, it was late on Sunday afternoon and we were in the car, winding our way back to Oxford. As a treat, and to delay the inevitable, we took a different route back, on smaller, more scenic back roads. The hedgerows loomed above us like foliage giants. I was going to miss this in a few months when I would be forced to return to Toronto. Suddenly Simon's words came back to me and I realized he knew me well; I was already fretting about leaving England. I shuddered as I attempted to shake the depressing thoughts and Oliver noticed.

"Everything all right?"

"Yes," I lied. "Just a bit chilly."

He reached into the back and pulled his sport coat forward. I took it from him and leaned forward to slip into the sleeves.

"Thank you. You're so sweet."

"It may seem gallant but it's really self-serving. If you catch a chill that could adversely affect our lovemaking. And I don't want to waste one glorious minute with you, darling."

I laughed. There were times when Oliver's words sounded like dialogue in a film.

"So I take it you wouldn't love me if I showered you with moist, mucousy kisses?" I asked in a nasal voice.

He chuckled. "Moist I like. Mucous I'm less fond of."

"Good to know."

"I believe in absolute honesty."

I paused for a second. "In the spirit of absolute honesty, can I ask you something, Oliver?"

"Of course."

"What are your plans? I mean, where will you be, say, next year? Do you know yet?"

He sighed. "Well, just before we left, I was in a meeting where we discussed the progress we'd made on the project and expectations for the rest of my secondment."

"And ..."

"We're actually ahead of schedule on the original mandate. A few other milestones have been added, so it looks like my time in London will be extended until January or February."

"Oh."

"Is that 'Oh, good' or 'Oh, not so good'?"

"Neither. I'm just surprised."

He turned to look at me. "I was going to tell you but I thought that you deserved a weekend where you could simply enjoy yourself, with little talk of the future, given the circumstances."

"I did have a wonderful weekend."

"If you'd like to talk about the future ..."

For a moment, the offer hung in the air. "No. I think I just want to bask in the glow of the loveliest weekend I've ever had. Thank you."

"It was my pleasure, I assure you."

"I've never learned how to be in the moment. This weekend came as close as ever."

"It's a handy skill to acquire, Lily."

"I'm coming to see that."

He reached for a CD and popped it into the car stereo. Another signature tune from the sixties began. One hand on the wheel, he raised his other hand to caress my cheek. I sighed.

"Mmmmm ..."

"My sentiment exactly," he said. "Close your eyes and just absorb it."

For once, I surrendered and obeyed.

Oliver had to return to London straightaway so we didn't get a chance to discuss anything more that evening. The next day, I went to the office as usual and took solace in my latest project. My goal was to finish the research and draft the article before I had to leave Oxford in seven weeks. With Simon now in Manchester and seeing Oliver only on weekends, I was remarkably productive. As September rolled into October, the latest crop of applications began to appear. Once again, the cycle of hope and uncertainty began. Walking to the City Centre one day I wondered how many thousands of students had experienced the very same feeling since the university first became a seat of higher learning in the twelfth century.

A few days before my scheduled departure, my colleagues at the Unit took me out to dinner. It was a bittersweet occasion. I knew that I might never see some of these people again. It all depended on the Fates. As I sat in the little French bistro on Little Clarendon, amidst the wine, food and laughter, I recalled at least four such dinners I attended for other scholars at the Unit. Only a lucky few would get to stay in Oxford, most of us were just passing through.

Oliver had driven up to Oxford late the night before to take me down to London. He said it would be easier to catch the flight but I also think he understood how hard it was for me to leave. He took me to dinner and to the theatre and didn't once mention academia, for which I was grateful. I wasn't saying goodbye to him but I would be miles away from the excitement of London for the next few months.

Simon rang me on my mobile while I was waiting in the boarding area. Talking with Simon usually buoyed me up but this time, neither his wit nor Oliver's charm could shake my sense of failure. Arriving in Oxford, I believed that this was going to be like putting jet fuel into my career trajectory. I was more productive than most and focused on my future. But it took something other than publications, teaching experience, and networking to land a post. Although I couldn't put a name to that elusive entity, I sensed I would stubbornly spend the next few years trying to find out.

CHAPTER 19

I ARRIVED AT PEARSON AIRPORT IN TORONTO TWO YEARS LESS one day from the date I began my postdoc. No one was there to greet me. Of course, the only one of the three men in my life who was on the same continent was Greg. But I felt awkward about asking him to come pick me up because he was living with Sophia. I got the feeling that she wouldn't appreciate me asking and didn't want to hear him say that I was not a top priority. My ego couldn't take that.

The one concrete thing I did have was in my jacket pocket. Oliver had given me the key to his condo when we'd parted at Heathrow so I wasn't homeless in my own hometown. When I started to protest, he put a finger to my lips, pressed gently, and implored me to accept his offer.

"This isn't a sly marriage proposal," he said. "Furthermore, it's neither a handout nor a noose 'round your lovely, lovely neck. Please, Lily. The place is sitting empty, and you need a base to start the next phase of your life. When I'm back in Toronto in a few months, we can talk, discuss your future, my plans and see where things might go."

I swallowed my pride and did the sensible thing. Having collected my bags off the airport carousel, I was now in a cab with the window halfway down to get some fresh fall air, making good time on the Gardiner Expressway toward downtown.

Arriving at Oliver's condo, I was greeted by name by the concierge. I was impressed. He welcomed me to the building and said if I needed anything, just to call down to the desk. I took the elevator to the eleventh floor, turned the key and at once, felt right at home. Oliver had changed little since I'd last been in the suite, although I did notice a few new pieces of artwork on the walls. There was a large vase of flowers on the dining room table with a small card poking out from amidst the greenery. How quintessentially Oliver. I smiled and opened the card. It read, "*Mi casa e su casa,* Lily. Champagne on ice. Enjoy. Ring when you've had a rest. Love, O."

He really was class personified. Walking into the spotless kitchen, I opened the refrigerator to find it had been stocked with fresh fruits, vegetables and gourmet meals from a neighbourhood bistro. Turning my head, as promised, on the counter there was a bottle of champagne chilling in an Art Deco-style silver urn.

I took a deep breath, looked around and sighed. It was nice to be back, wonderful to be pampered and best of all, absolutely decadent to have nothing more to do today than to fall onto the softest bed imaginable for an afternoon nap. I felt like Goldilocks as I succumbed to the lure of an eiderdown duvet and pudding-soft feather pillows.

I spent the next month consumed with finding work. Although Oliver never mentioned anything about my paying for the flat, I felt the need to become self-sufficient as soon as possible. It would have been much easier if I could have just relaxed, but that wasn't me. I divided my time between searching the web for academic posts that would start the following year and reconnecting with former business colleagues to find work for the next few months. Fortunately, one of those phone calls landed me a short-term contract at a public relations firm. It got me out of the condo and meeting people, which were key because I knew that personal connections worked so much better than applying to anonymous job ads. With Oliver still in London for a few months, I also had a lot of time on my hands and spending all day and all night at home at my computer drained me of energy and good humour. When Oliver would ring, I would snap at him. He took it in stride and then I'd hang up, feeling guilty for being so mean-spirited. He was wise enough to see my bad temper was existential but I was sure he was secretly relieved that I was miles away when I was stressed and bitchy.

Autumn passed quickly. I was in email contact with Simon weekly and I lived vicariously through him. Manchester was perfect for him and he was putting the Beale stamp on the department already. He had also met someone, although he wasn't forthcoming on details. All I knew was that his lover was originally from France and was, in Simon's words, "disarmingly gorgeous". Try as I might to get more details, I was stymied. His lone comment was, "Early days yet, El. Don't want to jinx it."

As for Greg, I contacted him by email a couple of weeks after I returned to Toronto and he replied almost immediately. We tried to set up a lunch date, but his shifts at the plant made it impossible for the first month and then he and Sophia were going away for a two-week vacation. The earliest we could get together was in early December. For that I was grateful; I didn't want to see him before I had more work lined up.

I had a lot of time to myself. My book manuscript had been edited and I'd made the necessary changes; I was now in the process of waiting for the publisher to see it through to printing, likely in the spring. I devised a budget that I could stick to through the spring and summer and spent time reading things other than material related to my research for the first time in years. Oliver subscribed to various magazines including *The New Yorker* and *The Economist*. I was also planning for the holidays. Oliver suggested I fly over to London but I suggested we get away on this side of the Atlantic. I chose San Francisco. The plan was that he would fly directly there two days before Christmas and I would fly out to meet him. I was so pleased to be getting away from the Toronto chill.

Two weeks before I was scheduled to meet up with Oliver, I was eating a green curry take-away dinner and checking my email on my laptop after work, when I got an email from one of the other Toronto universities. There were two evening half courses in need of an instructor. I had sent in a blanket application at the start of term, but due to my lack of seniority was assigned nothing. Now it seemed the original instructor bowed out at the last minute and because I'd maintained contact since I'd returned to Toronto, the deputy chair emailed me. This was encouraging. My other work contract was due to end in ten days in any case, and two more courses would look good on my CV. I replied immediately and the contract was emailed to me, signed and sent back within twenty-four hours.

Of course, I shared my good news with Oliver. He seemed a bit reserved in his congratulations. I knew he was thinking that this was a stop-gap measure and that I was still thinking that an academic post was likelier to get than an industry position. Because I would be seeing him soon, the conversation quickly turned to how we would spend our holiday week together. I also rang Simon. He would understand.

"Well done, my dear," were Simon's first words.

"I figure it's one way to work towards a stronger application."

"Absolutely. You must also make yourself indispensable to the organization from day one. That is, if you could envision yourself at that uni until you're a wizened old hag."

"You make it sound so appealing," I said.

"Gets the point across though, eh?"

"I guess."

"Have you shared your news with the other member of our trio?"

"Oliver?"

"How quickly we forget. I meant Master Gregory."

"No."

"Why not?"

"I haven't had a chance, and we're supposed to meet up for lunch in a few days anyways."

"Hmm … Anything you're not telling me?"

God, he could read me like a book. "I don't want to interfere."

"With what?"

"With him. And Sophia."

He laughed. "I cannot imagine that the vile seductress would or could keep her man away from his friends."

"Yeah, well …"

"Methinks you don't want to get any inkling our dear Gregory has moved on."

"Oh, shut up."

His voice softened. "Lily darling, have some faith. Anyway, I have something to tell you so make a polite query about my life."

I was delighted to change the subject. "Okay smart ass, what's new with you? A promotion? Another award? Finish another book?"

"Nothing relating to my professional life."

"With you, that's all there is," I said. But then I realized how churlish that sounded. "Sorry Simon. I don't usually wake up on the bitchy side of the bed."

"I don't maintain statistics, but ..."

"Are you keeping count?" We both laughed. Then it struck me. "Are you ill?"

"Never better."

I let out a long sigh. "Okay then, coy boy. What gives?"

There was a pause then spoke each word distinctly. "I'm in love."

"What?"

"It is possible."

I laughed. "Of course it is. But who? How?"

"You will recall that I alluded to a certain 'special someone'? Well, I wasn't sure if this was just a dalliance or something more, so I was hesitant to talk about him. Well, it turns out we're compatible, very compatible, and not just physically."

"Does Mr. Compatibility have a name?"

"He does. Jean-Marc."

"Sounds delicious."

"He is. He really is. He's also intelligent, charming and well-read."

"Is he on faculty?"

"No. He's a chef and has a bistro. In Manchester."

"Did you meet there?"

"We did. I went for dinner with friends and stayed for breakfast ... *a deux.*"

"An unusually quick courtship," I said.

"You know me. I'm not renowned for my spontaneity, but this was extraordinary. We've been together for one month and he is remarkable."

"When will I meet him?"

"Why don't you pop over for the holidays? We're doing an Oscar

Wilde-themed gift swap this year. Then Jean-Marc is taking me off to Paris for New Year's Eve *en français*."

"I can't. Oliver is meeting me in San Francisco."

"Fair trade. Hmm, let me think." He paused. "There is a conference in the summer here, in Manchester. The submission deadline is mid-February. You could submit a paper."

I thought about that. "Sure. Sounds like a plan."

"Good. I miss seeing your cheery visage almost daily."

"I'm sure Jean-Marc takes the edge off your pining for me."

"Discretion does not permit me to comment."

I laughed. "Ever the diplomat and the randy old boy, eh?"

"Guilty as charged."

"Well you've motivated me, Simon. I'll take a look at the conference website, see what they want for papers and submit something today."

"Who knows where that might take you?"

"At the very least, I'll get to see your cheery visage again and meet the fellow who has stolen your heart."

"I seem to be losing organs at an alarming rate."

"Well, at least this time it's less painful," I said.

"Indeed, it is. And do give my best to Gregory when you see him."

"Of course. Can I tell him your latest news?"

"Yes, yes," he said, followed by an intake of breath that was audible over the phone. "I can't believe it – for the first time since we three met, we are all in relationships. Oh, we're becoming so annoyingly provincial!"

"You, my friend, will never be provincial. You may spend summers in Provence, perhaps, but you will never be provincial."

"You're right. Well, enjoy 'Frisco. And my best to Oliver, too."

I wanted to tease him "Your best what?"

He volleyed right back. "Oh, if only Oliver were gay, I'd definitely give him my best ..."

"Back off there, Delilah. You've got your own man now!"

"Just making sure that you aren't taking anyone for granted. Good luck with the courses. And take care, dearest."

"You, too." I rang off.

He was right. All three of us had partners. Would wonders never cease?

Talking with Simon righted my mood. I smiled at the thought of him in love. I'd never seen him in a long-term relationship and the idea was strangely calming. He was a driven soul but beneath the staunch English reserve beat a heart that was sincere and kind. I was intrigued to meet the man who had so enchanted Simon, but that would have to wait until I could get back to England.

A few days later, I did meet up with Greg in a bistro on Charles Street, not far from the university. The place had been our student late-night haunt. It was open twenty-four hours and had a great banana chocolate cake.

Greg looked as handsome as ever, a tad older with flecks of grey in his hair, or perhaps it was just my imagination. For a split second I worried about how to greet him; all the awkwardness of what had happened in Toronto came back to me but Greg made my trepidations disappear. He bounded up the stairs of the bistro, smiling, and hugged me before I could embarrass myself by holding out my hand to shake his.

"It's so good to see you."

I sighed. "You too."

"Let's go in. I'm starved."

He held the door open and we went in, up the stairs and sat down at a table.

"How are you settling in?" he asked.

"Fine. I've just finished a contract and I'll be teaching two courses next term."

"That's great."

"Thanks. And you?"

"Well, before you ask, the dissertation has been on hold. Too much work. I mean, I've been working at the plant too much to concentrate on the PhD. But don't worry. I'll get back to it. Later."

I wasn't in a strong position to lecture him so I just nodded.

He pursed his lips. "I've disappointed you, I know."

"Don't be ridiculous."

"Lil, I know you too well – but less about me. What great plans do you have up your sleeve?"

One of two topics I'd been dreading – at least we'd get it off the table early.

"The courses should bolster my CV and the book is due in the spring. Other than that I'm applying all over the place."

"Even to colleges in smaller towns?" he asked, smiling.

"Some. But I'm still concentrating on the big city universities."

It was his turn to be respectfully silent.

"What are you doing for the holidays?" I asked.

"Staying home. Sophia just got a promotion. We hoped to get away for a week, but now she's keen to settle into her new role before going off somewhere. And you?"

"Oliver is flying over and we're going to meet in San Francisco."

He whistled. "Lucky lady. Seems you scored. You have a man who adores you and who can sweep you off to cool places."

"Speaking of people who are being swept away, guess who also has a man who adores him?"

Greg pondered for only a second. "No way. Scholar Simon has a beau?"

"Seems so."

"Well, well, pulled his nose out of the books for a minute, eh," Greg said.

"Don't know if it was his nose that sealed the deal."

"Lily Halton. Keep it clean, will you."

We both laughed.

"Where did they meet? Don't tell me in the archives," Greg said.

"Nope. Jean-Marc is a chef. He runs a bistro in Manchester."

"Too bad they didn't hook up when we were all in the same city. Gourmet dinner parties every weekend."

"If only they lived closer."

"Yeah. Would be nice, wouldn't it?"

The waiter came by at that point and we ordered drinks, a glass of chardonnay for me and a beer for him. Greg's next question floored me.

"Would you do something for me?"

"Sure. So long as it's legal and I'm not naked." I meant it as a joke but it came off strained as soon as the words left my lips. Sometimes I should just play it straight, I told myself. But Greg was polite and just pressed on.

"Lily ..." He paused. "I'm going to ask Sophia to marry me. I wonder if you might be my best person?"

Bingo! The second topic I'd been dreading.

"I'll understand if you think it's weird, a woman standing up for a guy. Then again, it is the twenty-first century."

"Best person?" I asked. "Ummm. Sure. I mean, of course. Sorry, I mean congratulations, Greg."

He looked relieved. I was still absorbing what he'd just asked.

"That's great," he said. "I'm sorry to spring this on you, but with all of your travel and job hunting, I wanted to be sure that you would be willing and free to do it."

I couldn't stop myself. "Is Sophia … is she okay with this?"

"Sure. She knows what you mean to me. I mean, that we're good friends. You know me better than anyone else."

"Does she know about … ?"

He paused. "Yes. I told her."

"And?"

"She's had lovers, too. That's all in the past. For both of us."

I paused to digest his reply. "When is the wedding?"

"Oh yeah," Greg laughed. "Not until the summer. We'd originally wanted September or October, but then I thought if you were teaching that would be hard for you. And for Simon. So we shifted it to August. That works better for Sophia in her new job anyway. Are you okay with August?"

For a second I heard it as if he were asking me about August as if we were planning our wedding. I shook it off.

"August. Sure," I said. "Of course I'll be there."

"Do you think Simon will come?"

"Absolutely." I tried another feeble joke. "Unless he's on his honeymoon."

Greg laughed. "Or you might be on your honeymoon. A little bird told me about rekindling your romance with Oliver in the UK."

"Yeah?"

"I'll see if I can convince Sophia to have a triple ceremony," he said, raising his glass. "Wouldn't that be a hoot?"

"Yeah," I lifted my glass out of reflex and he clinked his glass to mine. "A hoot."

Mercifully, the waiter came by to take our lunch order. My appetite was gone. I barely remember picking at my pasta, which tasted like moist strips of drywall covered in red sauce. Everything was changing so fast and I wasn't keeping pace. I just wanted to escape. Thank God for Oliver and for San Francisco in two weeks.

CHAPTER 20

I MADE IT THROUGH THE HOLIDAYS JUST FINE. OLIVER WAS GENerous and charming as always. The delights of San Francisco and wine country were also fantastic. When we got back to Toronto, there was a postcard from Simon, postmarked Paris, as well as a Christmas card from the other happy couple, Greg and Sophia. I felt like I was watching Noah pack the ark, checking off the pairs on a clipboard list.

After Oliver returned to London, I got into a groove, teaching, doing a bit of freelancing, and researching a paper that I hoped to present in Manchester that summer. It felt good to be productive. There were more job postings as winter turned to spring and I was relentless combing through the offerings. Despite my growing file of FOAD letters, I sent off another group of applications. I didn't want to miss my destiny.

Oliver finished his secondment in mid-March and returned to Toronto. At first, we kept up an unsustainable rhythm of lovemaking and him treating me like a goddess. As my teaching term wound down, I became more anxious about what I would be doing next, and my bitchy meter, as Simon would call it, was in the red zone most of the time. Oliver quickly learned to give me a wide berth. This distance was a relief for me, because being with him reminded me how far I lagged behind. But it was also distressing to me, because I sensed that he felt as helpless as I did. If I had full-time work, this would all disappear. I hated what was happening to me and to us.

Greg wrote the occasional email with details on the wedding plans. I still couldn't believe he was getting married. To me, it had all happened so fast. Simon had been asked to edit a volume on Newton's *Principia*. My book was still due to come out, but now the publisher had shifted the launch from spring to fall.

The one event on my horizon that I was looking forward to was the Manchester conference. Oliver asked if I wanted him to accompany me, but I said it might be better if I went over alone. A few days before I was scheduled to leave, as we sat side by side on his leather couch, drinking coffee, I felt obliged to explain.

"I know this ... me ... my situation has made me tough to live with," I said. "I'll be staying with Simon and Jean-Marc. Not really the kind of accommodations you're used to. And I'll be either busy or exhausted. I've got to spend my time networking. And then come back to do whatever there is to do to be a good 'best person' for Greg."

"Are you sure you wouldn't like me to come?" Oliver leaned over to whisper in my ear as he massaged my shoulders. "We could get away for a wee break after the conference. Mallorca or perhaps Belgium?"

I pulled away so I could face him. "You're so sweet and I've been such a horrible bitch. No. I can't ... I don't think I deserve it. I haven't worked enough to get a break from anything."

"Lily. You're still young ..."

"I'm thirty-six and unemployed and ..."

"Underemployed," he interjected.

"I don't give a damn how you parse it, Oliver. I'm overeducated, underemployed and living off my boyfriend. It's a wonder I can look myself in the mirror most mornings."

"Look for full-time work, then."

"So give up on the PhD?"

"You earned the PhD. No one is asking you to give that up. But go back to industry."

"That's what you always figured, didn't you?"

"What are you talking about, Lily?"

"You always thought this PhD was a dalliance. A hobby. That one day I'd come to my senses ..."

"I had no qualms about you pursuing a doctorate. I just mentioned the fact that tenure-track jobs are scarce and becoming more so. I know your potential and hate to see you waste it."

"Oh, thank you, Svengali."

"Lily ..."

"Look. I'm trying my best. I realize I'm not the perfect little consort. I'm sorry that sitting around, primping and preening and waiting to hear about your productive professional day isn't enough for me. Maybe you should have chosen more wisely."

"I adore you."

"Well, that isn't enough for me."

The room was perfectly still. The twinkling lights of the city below were the only sign of life at that moment. I took a deep breath before I spoke next.

"Oliver. I need some fresh air."

He moved off the couch. "That's a wonderful idea. Let's go for a walk."

"No. I need to be alone. I need to think."

He looked at me his brows together, his lips pinched.

"Don't worry. I'm a big girl. I'll be back after I've cleared my head."

He nodded. I put on my shoes, grabbed a jacket from the hall closet and my keys and left the suite. I had the palpable urge to run away, but I had nowhere else to go.

The conference in Manchester gave Oliver and me some distance from each other. I convinced myself that giving another paper was a step in the right direction for my career and therefore justified the expense of the flight and conference fees. I saved lodging costs by accepting Simon's standing offer of a place to stay. That also gave me a chance to meet Simon's partner.

Jean-Marc was charming, gracious and a talented chef. Having studied at the Cordon Bleu school and having worked for a decade in fine hotels, he had spent the past five years establishing two bistros in Manchester. Simon had managed to successfully balance his academic career with nurturing a relationship that obviously suited him. It was inspiring to see how two people, with different cultural and occupational backgrounds, openly supported and learned from each other. There was no sense of competition or divisiveness. And the bond was not only a sexual one. Simon was still Simon, and he now he had someone in his life with whom he could share the day-to-day triumphs and setbacks as well as future plans. Although they hadn't been together that long, it was as if they had known each other all their lives. More than once, watching them work together in the kitchen or when we all went shopping together, I wondered why I couldn't seem to get to that point with Oliver.

The day before I was to return to Toronto, Simon and I went out alone for tea and I asked him. "What's wrong with me?"

"I beg your pardon?"

"You and Jean-Marc get along so well. You're an academic. He's a chef. You're English. He's French. There are so many differences between you two and yet you get along like ... like ..."

"Yes?"

"Well, you know what I mean," I said. "Oliver and I should be just like you two. But lately we've been fighting. No. I've been fighting with him. He's been so good to me, and I just rip his head off. And I can't help it."

"What does he say, El?"

"Not much. I think he's bewildered by my outbursts. I don't understand them myself."

"Is he pressuring you?"

"Not at all."

"Are you pressuring yourself?"

"What do you mean?"

"Well, are you expecting something more of yourself than you currently have?"

"Someone better than Oliver?"

"No. I mean the total package. The man, the home, the job."

I looked at him. "If you're asking if I'd like to be working full-time, then the answer is, 'Yes!' of course."

"Are you taking out your frustrations on Oliver because you're not working full-time?"

"No. Yes. Maybe."

"It sounds as if you, my dear, are embroiled in existential inner conflict."

"Thank you, Dr. Freud."

"I adore you, dearest, but I must say that you are not easy to be with when your life is in limbo. You are used to achieving and moving forward. Stasis is not an optimal state of being for you, and those who try to help are not welcome."

Simon had never said anything like that before to me. "Are you saying that I'm hard to be with when things don't go my way?"

He paused and I thought he was going to deny it. "It's more specific than that. You expect so much of yourself that when you're thwarted, whether by your own actions or circumstance, you let self-doubt take you on a downward spiral."

I sat there, mouth agape, taking in Simon's words. He reached across the table and, taking both of my hands in his, looked me square in the eyes. When I tried to avert my gaze, two fingers came up to pivot my face so I couldn't escape his eyes.

"El, don't push everyone away. We're just trying to help. To be there for you like you've been there for us. I adore you because of who you are, not what you do or some ridiculous title."

I could feel tears threatening to topple my resolve.

"But ... but ... it wasn't supposed to be like this."

"I know, darling."

"I feel like such a failure. I've wasted so much time."

Simon tipped his head. "Was coming to Oxford a waste of time?"

I paused a moment. "Of course not."

"And you'll always have your book."

"If it's ever ..."

"*When* it's published."

"I guess."

"Uncle Simon is never wrong."

I laughed.

"Uncle Simon may not be as modest a friend as some others," he said. "But he is a man of great taste, in clothing, in lovers, and in friends. I don't keep company with failures, *ergo,* you cannot possibly be a failure, El. You are merely going through a rough patch so take the help that's offered."

"I suppose you're right. Again."

"Of course I am. Remember, what doesn't kill you, makes you stronger."

I laughed. "Is that your best closing line?"

He leaned back in his chair and smiled. "No. Believe it or not, being in love has made me uncharacteristically scatterbrained. So my closing line is actually a desperate plea."

"Oh, don't tell me you want me to be best person at your wedding, too."

He laughed. "No. I am so embarrassed to ask this of you, my dear. Would you pick up the chit for tea? I forgot my wallet at the flat."

"Of course you silly git," I said, tears forgotten as I reached into my pocket.

The combination of Simon's pep talk, giving a solid paper at the conference and getting away buoyed my spirits so that when Oliver met me at Pearson Airport, I think he was shocked at how much my mood had changed. For the better part of the next few weeks, we lived together with no quarrels. Most of my time was taken up with making sure I didn't miss any last minute posts and with helping Greg. Helping the groom was, as I learned first-hand, far less taxing than being a bridesmaid or maid of honour. He was so easygoing and left most of the major decisions to Sophia so my main role was to serve as sounding board and friend.

I was glad that I didn't have to spend too much with Sophia – not that she wasn't nice to me but because I felt like a third wheel when she, Greg and I were together. It was strange that being part of a trio with Simon and Greg was fine, but another woman was a hard pill for me to swallow.

Because Greg didn't want a stag party, I was off the hook for planning what would have been, for me, a truly surreal event. Instead, I arranged an evening out at a high-end pool parlour and restaurant one week before the wedding. There were about thirty guys there, most of them from the plant, and I had a fantastic time as the only woman. Throughout the evening, I caught Greg watching me but I didn't say anything to him until we met up days later to discuss final wedding arrangements.

"So, boss," I asked, "everything on course?"

"You bet."

"Any prohibitions on what I can say in my speech?"

Greg paused for a second. "Nope. I believe in absolute honesty."

"Really?"

"What's that supposed to mean?" he asked.

"Just that total honesty has been known to get a man in trouble now and again."

"Okay. I don't mean when your wife asks you, 'Do I look fat in this?'"

I laughed. "Glad I'll never face that problem!"

Greg smiled. "Yeah, but you'll have other challenges."

"Like what?"

"Hmmm ... how your partner takes it when other guys ogle you."

I exploded with laughter.

"What's so funny, Lil?"

"I can't believe you used the word ogle. You sound like my grandmother."

"Okay, when guys stare at your ass or your ..."

"I get it."

"Like at the pool hall."

"What are you talking about?"

"Those guys from the plant weren't looking at your brains. Their eyes were fixated further south."

"And how would you know?"

"I'm your friend. I was watching out for you."

"Keeping me safe from?"

"Them. Yourself."

I smiled. "Oh, really."

"I'm just saying that I recognized the fact that you were the only woman among a pack of ..."

"Wolves?"

"Men."

"And?"

"And I didn't want to see any behave badly. They're great guys but I couldn't predict if they could ..."

"Keep their hands to themselves?"

"I was going to say if they could resist you. You're smart, everyone knows that, but you're a fox, too. And I don't think you see that in yourself. Add liquor and I'm just glad that the evening ended without ..."

"Without you having to defend my honour, Lancelot?"

"Sure."

That was so typical of Greg. "Well, thanks."

"No thanks needed, milady."

I decided to tease him a bit. "But it might have been fun. How often does a girl get the chance to have a go with four or five guys at once?"

"Lil."

"It would make a great story for when I'm old and grey in the seniors' home."

"You talk a big game but we both know that you're a one-man woman."

"Do we now?" I asked.

"You and I are cut from the same cloth."

"I'm not getting married."

"Yet," he said.

"We'll see." I was getting uncomfortable with the conversation so I decided to change the subject. "Let's talk about your wedding."

"Like I said, everything is ready to go. Ceremony on the island, then dinner at the yacht club. Not my idea but Sophia's parents are keen. When does Simon get in?"

"They're supposed to be here tomorrow evening," I said.

"It'll be great to see him and to meet Jean-Marc."

"He wrote you, eh? He said he was going to apologize for missing your non-stag party."

"Are they staying with you?" Greg asked.

"No. Oliver offered but they said they'd made reservations at a bed and breakfast near the village. Jean-Marc has friends in Toronto so they're staying close to them."

"Sounds good."

"Well, having read up on the duties of a best person, I think now is as good a time as any to pass along words of wisdom."

"Okay. Don't ..."

"No, you goof ball. From me to you."

He leaned back in his chair and put his arms behind his head. "Okay, bestie. Fire away."

I stopped for a moment to look at him. He was single for the next two days. Questions fluttered through my mind. How long before he became a father? How often would we see each other? Would I ever marry? Would this be the last time we'd meet, just the two of us, to talk about everything or nothing in particular, with such ease?

"I'm ready," he said, breaking through my reverie.

"Hmmm … I think I can sum it all up by saying, don't forget to be nice to yourself."

He tipped his head to look at me at an angle.

"I mean, don't let anyone, I mean any woman, take advantage of you," I said.

"I'll do my best."

"Good." I didn't know where else to go, what else to say.

Luckily, I was rescued by the waitress, who came by with the bill.

Greg picked up the tab and smiled as he pulled out his wallet. "And, no, I don't think you're taking advantage of me."

The ceremony was beautiful. The weather was perfect, warm and sunny with a breeze off the lake. The whole day was a combination of tradition and relaxed informality. There was no head table. Simon, Jean-Marc and Oliver joined the wedding party at their table and I can't remember when I laughed so much. At Sophia and Greg's request, speeches were kept short and sweet to maximize time for dancing. All too soon, the evening was over. The newlyweds set off for an airport hotel; they were scheduled to fly to Bora Bora for a ten-day honeymoon the next day. Simon and Jean-Marc planned to meet Oliver and me for a late brunch the next morning at Oliver's condo; Jean-Marc had offered to cook for us. Riding home in the taxi I realized that, come Monday morning, I had no appointments to keep, no work to do. I closed my eyes and shut out that disturbing thought. I'd deal with it on Monday.

CHAPTER 21

THE MONDAY AFTER GREG'S WEDDING WAS THE LOW POINT OF MY life. I realized I had been in graduate school or living on the margins of the academic life for an entire decade. If it weren't so pathetic, I might have laughed. Lying around the condo in my bathrobe, reviewing my life as it had diverted so far off course, I made a mental list of all the things that were missing. I did chuckle at one point – when I rhymed off the list, it sounded like alternative lines to that 1980 Vapors tune, 'Turning Japanese':

> 'No sex, no job, no hubby, no house,
> No pension, no car, no wonder my future
> looked dark.'

Our sex life had reached a nadir. It wasn't that I didn't care; it was that I couldn't figure out how to change things. I felt I had no control. I had become an absolute bitch, to the point that Oliver was in a tough spot; he wanted to help, but I consistently railed at his suggestions, so he became silent and that pissed me off even more.

The day after Thanksgiving, Oliver was at the office when a

special delivery package arrived addressed to me. I didn't recognize the address of the sender. I tried to pry open the large staples that held the corrugated cardboard together but they wouldn't budge. After swearing a blue streak, I went into the kitchen to find scissors. Finding none, I grabbed a sharp knife and went back into the living room. I slid the blade under an offending staple. As I struggled to jimmy it open, the knife slipped as the staple popped open. It all happened in slow motion. The blade glanced off the hand that had been steadying the box and I dropped the knife immediately. A second later I was bleeding. I stood there, slowly dripping blood on the box. Snapping out of my short stupor, I ran to the bathroom, grabbing a tea towel and pressing it hard to my crimson palm.

"Shitty, shit, shit!"

This was the icing on the cake. I was pretty sure I wasn't going to bleed out but I didn't know if I would need stitches. In the bathroom, I tore apart the cupboard contents. At a glance, I couldn't find any gauze or bandages. It was so like Oliver never to need bandages. I glanced at my hand and it was still bleeding.

"Screw it," I said, as I found a package of my sanitary napkins. I might be stupid but I was also resourceful. Clawing at the package with my good hand until one napkin fell out, I snatched the bloody tea towel, tossed it in the sink, then clamped the napkin on the cut and plopped down on the edge of the tub, resting my head against the cool tiled wall. I sat there to catch my breath, hand raised higher than my heart like I'd learned in First Aid class decades before. The napkin wasn't saturated, so I knew I'd live. It made me queasy to split open straight cuts. Even paper cuts made me weak-kneed if I opened them, so I steeled myself to take one look to see if the cut was deep. I was no real doctor, but I couldn't see tendons or open vessels, so I pressed the napkin back to the cut and, holding my wound and napkin tight against my chest, calmly began to look again for a bandage. Sure enough, in the medicine cabinet there was a box of BandAids of various sizes that I'd missed before. Slipping the box under one arm, I opened the box one-handed and spilled the contents onto the counter so I could choose the appropriate size.

With the cut neatly bandaged and curious about the package that started it all, I went back into the living room. Opening the flaps, drops of blood staining the box, I laughed so hard, tears started to form. The box was filled with copies of my published book. I picked up a copy and was struck by the irony of it all: fresh blood, moist tears, and years of sweat.

By January, I was a wreck. My hand had healed perfectly, but Oliver and I were barely talking. I was consumed by a feeling of betrayal that the one thing I'd done right, publishing my book, had been met with absolute indifference by the academy. No reviews. No book launch. I was so sensitive to any setback that I withdrew from all but the most basic contact with friends. Greg was busy setting up house with Sophia, but when he called I let the answering machine pick up. Even Simon, with whom I had stopped talking regularly by phone or Skype, had contacted Oliver to ask if I was away or ill.

I couldn't continue like this, but I didn't know how to break the cycle. It all came to a head one day. I was sitting at the computer, wasting time, as usual. Having been away on business for a week, Oliver turned his key in the door, dropped his bag and came over to kiss me. I pulled away.

"Are you all right?" he asked.

"Are you all right? What the hell do you think?"

He sighed. "Bad day, I see."

"Bad year, more like it."

"Oh Lily."

"Oh Lily, what? It'll get better? Don't worry? You've got me?"

"I wasn't going to say that."

"Fine. How about, 'Do you like being a kept woman?'"

"I've never said that. And I never thought that."

"Yeah, well what about what I've thought?"

"I wouldn't know," he said. "You haven't been very communicative and I'm not a mind reader."

"The man can't read minds. Woohoo. He is a mere mortal, after all."

"What's that supposed to mean?"

I laughed. "Christ, Oliver, you've got it all. A great condo. A fantastic career. Anything you want, you can get. Life is bloody grand for you."

"So why not help me enjoy it?"

"You really don't get it, Sherlock. I don't want to be your anonymous, vacuous, plus one. I don't want to sit here and wait for you to come home so you can tell me the fascinating things you've been up to. I want to do my own fascinating things."

"And you shall."

"Bullshit! What have I done since I came back to Toronto?"

He just stood there. I interpreted the silence to mean he had no answer, not that he was afraid to comment.

"Exactly. Nothing. *Nada*. Sweet fuck all!" I said.

He took a deep breath and then spoke softly. "What can I do?"

My next words surprised me. "Kick me out of this soft cushy nest. Let me go."

"Where?"

"I've got to figure that out for myself."

"Lily, come on. We're both exhausted. Let's go to bed and tackle this together in the morning."

"We can't fix this. I need to start fresh. I need to regain my self-respect and I can't do it by sitting around here on my ass, day after day, deluding myself into believing I'll get an academic post."

"But ..."

I got up from the couch, walked straight up to him and kissed him softly on the lips. "I don't want us to end up hating each other. I've been enough of a bitch. I wish it could have been different. You were right. I should never have changed careers. It was an insane idea that's cost me more than I can stand."

"Where will you go?" he asked.

"This weekend I'll find my own place. It's a start. Then I'll *have* to find work."

"Lily, I wish ..."

I put one finger to his lips. "I wish, too."

True to my word, I moved out of his gorgeous condo that weekend into an old, plain one-bedroom walk-up apartment near Old Mill station. I chose that location both because it was inexpensive and because I didn't want to run into Oliver. The temptation to go back to him and an easy but soul-destroying life of dependency was too strong.

I spent the next three months looking for a public relations or communications position. I had a number of interviews but it took until April before I landed a good position with a research institute on University Avenue. It was a new post, so I had no predecessor and doing communications for scientists meant I was in my element while they were thrilled to be left to their area of expertise in pure research.

In his indomitable style, Oliver sent flowers every day after I left. I sent emails, once a week, telling him I was fine and asking him to give me space. We met once for lunch just after I landed my new job. He was charming and good company as always. As we sipped coffees, having finished dessert, he asked if we could meet for dinner the following evening.

"I don't think that's a good idea," I said.

"I see my charm is wearing off," he joked.

"No. Never. It's me."

"How *cliché*."

"I know it sounds worn, but I've had some time to think it over and I think that you know me too well. You and I … we're fantastic in bed but …"

"Yes?"

"You're set. You've made your mark. I'm not even close."

"So let me help you."

"I'm not looking for a patron."

"What are you looking for, Lily?"

"First, I need to see where I'm headed. I don't need to be directed, or cajoled or drawn in. I need to … it sounds so California Zen master … I need to find me."

"How long do you think that journey will take?"

"No idea."

"Should I wait?"

"Do you think you'll live that long?" I joked.

He chuckled. "Much depends on a man's motivation. If you do need …"

"Are you asking to be my friend with benefits?"

"Perhaps." Then he shook his head. "No. I've been down that road before and …"

"See? That's what I meant. We're on different paths."

"Well, it was wonderful while it lasted."

"It was. And I shall always ...," I began to say.

This time he reached across the table to put his finger against my lips. There was nothing more to say.

After that lunch, Oliver stopped sending flowers and gave me what I'd asked for: time on my own. I threw myself into my work. It took longer than I'd expected to readjust to professional life. It was bizarre but I'd forgotten what it was like to wake up at seven every morning, to work as part of a team, and to earn two thousand dollars each week instead of every month.

With three months on my own under my belt, I decided that my life was turning around and I was ready to attempt to reconnect socially with my friends. I renewed regular email contact with Simon, chatting on weekends. When he asked if I'd spoken with Greg lately, I had to say 'No'. So as the days grew longer and warmer I finally picked up the phone at work and called the newlywed.

"Well, well. Is that my old pal, Lily 'The Hermit' Halton?"

"Yeah. I get it. How is marriage treating you?"

"It's good, thanks. How's the new job?"

"It was exactly what I needed."

"Do you miss the ivory tower?"

"Sometimes. It's hard to give up on the dream, on what you've worked towards. You know me. I'm stubborn."

He smiled. "Stubborn. Determined."

"And you know I'm not a morning person. Getting up early every day was tough at first."

"But the money's good, eh?"

"Much better than teaching one course."

"How's Simon?"

"Good. He's doing a lot of neat stuff in his new unit," I said. "He says hello."

"Are you going over to see him any time soon?"

"No. I might go to Vancouver for a symposium, for work, but nothing on the books for a trip to England. What about you?"

"Funny you should ask."

"Okay. Dish."

"Well, it's not England, but Sophia has got a great opportunity. A three-year gig in Singapore."

"Singapore?" I couldn't believe it. Just when I thought things were getting back to normal. I'd been counting on Greg and Sophia, if that was how it had to be, being part of my social core now that I was back in Toronto and moving on with my life.

"Yeah."

"And you're ..."

"Going along for the ride."

"What will you do there, Greg?"

"The company has lined up a contract for me, too. That was one of the conditions of her taking the job. A sort of spousal appointment, in academic lingo."

What could I say? "Congrats."

"Thanks."

"When do you leave?"

"In three weeks."

There was a long pause. I spat out the first thing that came into my head.

"Need help packing?"

He laughed. "Nope. The company pays for everything. We'll put our stuff in storage, and then we move into a furnished apartment. The pictures I've seen make it look really nice. The place has a pool and it's right in the city."

"Great."

"Sophia has meetings in London and Munich before we go on to Singapore, so we're flying the long way around. I'll email Simon. Maybe he can come down for a day and we can catch up. Any chance you could come over to London for a few days?"

"No. Work is consuming me right now. Amazing. London. Munich. Singapore. You've become a real globetrotter."

"Look who's talking." He paused. "I'll miss you, Lil."

I smiled. "Ah, three years will go by in a flash. I hear the food's great and you'll get to travel all over Southeast Asia. It's good to get out there. Simon's gone. I left for two years. It's your turn." As the words came out of my mouth, I only hoped he heard them as sincere; I was trying hard to make them sound that way.

CHAPTER 22

I WAS SO RELIEVED TO HAVE A FULL-TIME POSITION THAT SUMMER. My work colleagues became my main source of human contact and my projects replaced academic research as my main font of intellectual stimulation. I was also fortunate to work for a woman who challenged me while at the same time giving her entire team enough latitude to do our own research and work out problems independently. There was no micromanaging. She had brought together a group of smart, savvy, well-educated and ambitious people who pulled together when necessary and who toiled on their own equally well.

When the last FOAD letter arrived from my recent round of applications, I was momentarily surprised. Having shifted my focus, I'd almost forgotten that there was still one live application. As I held the thin envelope in my hand, I realized that my academic door was well and truly closed. That evening while relaxing after work, listening to a jazz CD with a glass of chilled white wine on the table, I sat down with the file of rejection letters. I flipped through page after page. There were letters from many of the leading universities from across North America and the UK. The phrases were different but each crisp white sheet had the same ultimate message: despite my achievements and stellar record, I wasn't their choice. I had never even been invited to an interview.

Picking up the whole pile and flipping through six years of correspondence, I shook my head. I had been keeping the file to make a collage when I finally got an academic post. It was going to be my revenge art, showcasing all the university logos on the letters along with photos of future award ceremonies, copies of multiple book contracts and magazine profiles, as if to say, "See what you could have had if you'd chosen me?" Now the file was just a reminder of years of wasted time. I added the final letter, closed the file, walked over to the recycling bin and pitched the whole lot.

The next year and a half went by faster than I could have imagined. Every fall I did feel an emotional tug when all the back to school commercials started but I chalked it up to a mix of habit and nostalgia. My life was much better now. I was still enjoying work at the research institute and with a promotion to VP Communications I felt I was more or less back on track professionally.

When my lease came up for renewal, I decided it was time to move back downtown. I found a great condo on Bay Street with a gym, pool and steps from hip restaurants and bars and a short walk to work. Having saved a tidy sum by living in my old sparse apartment, I was now ready and able to furnish my new place with better furniture. My goal was to look around to buy my own place as soon as possible so I'd have some equity. The Toronto real estate market was hot and I needed to jump on the property ladder before it was too late. Turning forty was staring me in the face.

I was also ready to start dating again. Simon helped me craft a catchy profile, which I posted on a couple of on-line dating sites. I was a bit wary at first, but soon learned that if I adjusted my expectations – not wanting to be married, pregnant and living in the suburbs within the next six months but just keen to meet interesting men – online dating was a pleasant diversion. If I met a fantastic guy, then fine, I'd consider a long-term relationship. If not, I was happy to date a string of guys that wouldn't cramp my style or dictate how I spent my time. I was concentrating on myself and it felt damn good.

When I chatted with Simon, it was obvious that he, too, was focused on building his professional reputation. Life with Jean-Marc was going well. They were two ambitious men in their thirties in a committed relationship, but both rising stars in two very different fields. I often wondered if I had met up with Oliver now, with both of us professionally successful, if our relationship might have survived, even thrived. I took full responsibility for being the person who had torpedoed us. Right people, wrong timing. How many other people had suffered the same fate?

As for Greg, he sent Simon and me cards on our birthdays, at Christmas and, funnily enough, for Canada Day. If I didn't know better, I'd have guessed he was homesick. I wondered if there was some critical point where the distance became so great that a person really was on the other side of the world. Although Simon and I had an ocean between us, we still talked regularly. Greg never called and Simon reported a similar radio silence. Maybe we'd reached that point in our lives where we'd drifted apart. Maybe it was a married guy thing or a heterosexual guy thing. I didn't get it but I didn't fight it, either.

By the time December rolled around again, I was in a groove. When Simon invited me to visit, as he had every year since I'd returned to Toronto, I decided this was the year to return to England.

I didn't want to spend another Christmas alone. I booked a Sunday evening flight, business class, so that I would arrive in London the morning of 20 December. Simon wanted to come down to London, both to meet me at Heathrow and to spend a few days in the city, shopping.

Luggage in tow, when I saw Simon leaning on the rail in Heathrow I had a sense of *déjà vu*. But this time, we were meeting as equals, not as Simon the tour guide and me as the newbie. When he saw me, he raised a small placard that read, "Welcome back to London, Lily. So glad you've been paroled." I laughed as I saw the reaction of my fellow travelers.

Simon looked a bit older, but as dashing and stylish as ever in skinny dark jeans, a crisp violet shirt and bone-coloured trench coat with a lime green cashmere scarf. After the hugs, he took my roller bag and we marched off to catch the Heathrow Express into the city. I had booked two rooms at The Paddington Hilton for three nights. That way we had the tube at our doorsteps and it was a short taxi ride to Euston to catch the train to Manchester.

Arriving at the hotel, we checked in and Simon kindly suggested I unpack and have a short nap to adjust to jet lag.

"I'll unpack this," he gestured to his overnighter, "and check up on email while you're resting. But be warned, you'll be shattered if you sleep too long in the middle of the day so I'll ring you in ninety minutes."

I saluted.

He placed one hand on each of my shoulders and spun me, one hundred eighty degrees. "On your way, errant colonial!"

What could I do but obey? True to his word, ninety minutes after I left him in the lobby, Simon rang me. It was two-thirty in the afternoon.

"Sleep well?" he asked.

"Yes."

"Shall we have tea downstairs? We can plan our assault on the shops and on London culture."

"Sounds divine."

"How long do you need to make yourself presentable? Half an hour?"

"What? Oh, sure. I can chisel the carbuncles and warts off in thirty minutes."

He laughed. "Most days I'm not aware of the age difference between us, El."

"It's just five years," I said.

"Well, I'm not looking forward to being forty."

"Simon, I've got to go otherwise I'll never be able to grind off the age spots before tea time."

"Right. Happy grinding." He hung up.

I was still smiling as I stepped into the shower. I missed being with him.

Catching up over tea and working out which shops and art galleries to visit, we spent a jam-packed three days in the city. London sparkled in December with twinkling lights on Oxford Street and people keen to celebrate the holidays. It was bewitching. Simon wanted to find gifts for Jean-Marc partly because Jean-Marc was a shameless snoop when it came to finding hidden presents. Being with Jean-Marc brought out a boyish quality I'd never noticed in Simon before. It was a joy to watch.

When I met Simon in the hotel lobby the day before we were to leave to go up to Manchester, I noticed something was wrong right away.

"What's wrong? Jean-Marc?"

"He's fine."

"Then what?"

"Our funding has been cut."

"At the unit?"

"Yes."

"What does that mean?" I asked.

"I've got a position for the rest of this academic year then I'm out. Two others, as well."

"Out?"

"Back on the job market. Bloody fine time to tell us," Simon said.

"I guess they wanted to give you as much time as they could."

"Small mercy."

"Did they give a reason?"

"Budget cuts. I know that political machinations are part of it but officially it's all about the numbers."

I hugged him. "I'm so sorry."

"Thanks, El. I shall survive. It's not a diagnosis of pancreatic cancer or a real beating." He put his hand where his spleen used to be.

"Oh, stop," I said. "Can you transfer to another department?"

"I don't know," he said. "Something will come up. In any case, I think I'm still in shock right now."

"Have you told Jean-Marc?"

"Not yet. It would just depress him. He doesn't understand how academia works and I don't want to worry him. He adores the holidays. I'll tell him after the break."

"You are so good," I said.

"I'm not going to let a small setback ruin our last evening in London either," he said, looping his arm through mine and we started walking.

"Where are we going?"

"Change of plans. We need some cheer. First drinks at the bar then off to confer with the concierge."

"Why?"

"What better to buoy the spirit than a good panto?"

"A what?"

"A holiday pantomime. Let's see if we can get tickets. If the panto is sold out, I know there's a Shakespearean tragedy in the West End. Nothing puts things into sharper perspective than watching someone else having a truly wretched day."

I laughed even as I envied Simon's confidence and resolve.

CHAPTER 23

SIMON LANDED ON HIS FEET. HARVARD UNIVERSITY HAD A tenure track position in History of Science for which he was more than qualified. When his post at Manchester ended in June, he and Jean-Marc rented a chateau in the south of France before Simon prepared to move to Boston. Jean-Marc could not leave his business right away, so for the first year of the Simon's two-year contract they resigned themselves to a long-distance relationship. Simon did, however, bring his latest project, the edited volume of Newton's *Principia,* which was well underway, to Boston.

Their ultimate goal was for Jean-Marc to train someone to take over the Manchester bistros and to come to the US, apply for the proper papers, and to open another bistro in Boston. Simon was optimistic that all of this would happen seamlessly.

By the time Simon was completing his first year at Harvard, I had celebrated my third year with the research institute. I had no intention of switching jobs, but when a head-hunter contacted me with an opportunity to join an international genomics consortium as the Executive Director of their Canadian office in Toronto it was too good an offer to refuse. In addition to the challenge and the promotion, there was also the tantalizing fact of more international travel. That was one of the things I enjoyed about the decade spent in academia – travel opportunities abounded, albeit on a lean budget. Travel on business, or even on vacations while working full-time, was exponentially better because I didn't have to count pennies before ordering meals, sleep in drafty dorms, or take dodgy flights to save money.

Whenever I booked a trip, I contacted friends to see if we might meet up; if I was lucky, we'd both be free and I could usually tack on a day of vacation with no problem. Sometimes there was no one in the cities I would visit. But invariably, as Simon had once said to me, I could tap into the network of friends and acquaintances that I had built up in graduate school and during my postdoctoral fellowship. That first year in my new position I logged trips to New York City, San Francisco, Santiago de Chile, Bologna, Paris, London and Zurich as well as Montreal and Vancouver so many times I lost count. I managed to catch up with three of my former MA colleagues. Janice, who had done her first degree in medical genetics, was actually working for a genomics research facility in Berkeley, California, and was married with two small children; Maggie and her partner Taryn were running an environmental NGO in Santiago de Chile; and Max, who started his PhD with Simon, Greg and me, was an administrator with Doctors Without Borders, based in Montreal, and divorced twice already. I learned that the other member of our MA cohort, Louis, was working for the Ministry of Natural Resources, doing research in Nunavut, but there was little chance of my visiting the far north for business.

When I met Janice, Maggie and Max they all asked if I kept in touch with anyone from the program. I told them the latest news on

Simon and that Greg was in Singapore for three years. Over lunch at her home in a suburb of Santiago, Maggie joked that she was surprised I wasn't in Singapore with Greg then apologized when I told her he was married to someone else.

"I always thought you two would get together," Maggie said. "He was so obviously crazy about you."

What could I say? "He's a great guy."

"If I was into men, I'd have jumped his bones in seconds."

"Really?"

"Come on. He was smart, nice, had the best hair and he was in pretty fine shape."

"I guess."

"Lily, woman should not live by bread or vibrators alone, at least not forever."

We both laughed. "Thanks for the tip, Maggie."

"Hey, it's great to catch up. I often wondered what became of everyone. It was a given that Simon would end up as a professor. What else would he do? It's his natural habitat."

"Yeah."

"We've all done okay, eh?"

"I suppose. It just took some of us a bit longer. Okay, a lot longer."

"Lily, don't beat up on yourself. You've got a great career. So what if you don't have two SUVs in the driveway or a closet full of thousand-dollar handbags? That's all bullshit."

"Thanks, Maggie."

She winked at me. "But if you'd snagged Greg, I might even envy you."

Maggie's words echoed in my head often and later that month, when I'd returned home, I emailed Greg. I told him about the new job, about meeting up with our former classmates and generally kept things light. I didn't mention what Maggie had said. I also told him I was traveling more in my new position and I would be in London next month. I left it at that. There was a reply in my mailbox within hours, despite the twelve hour time difference. He said Sophia also had a trip planned to London and he could accompany her. He ended his email with, "Looking forward to catching up. In person."

I was, too.

After a few more emails, Greg and I established that our time in London would overlap by one and a half days. We arranged to meet for lunch at one of my favourite restaurants in South Kensington, not far from the Natural History Museum. The restaurant, rumour had it, had been the meeting place for Polish resistance fighters and allied spies during the Second World War. During recent renovations, they uncovered some bullet holes and so they left them unplastered, on display under Plexiglas, to add mystery to the new ambience. I remembered the place because it had borscht and pierogies that were delicious.

A conference call made me twenty minutes late. Walking into the small restaurant, I spotted Greg. He was perusing the menu so he didn't notice me right away. He looked leaner, in an open-necked dress shirt and dark trousers, and his hair was a bit longer; other than that, he was the same old Greg. I smiled. It felt as if no time had passed at all. As I walked toward him, he looked up, grinned and got up to greet me with a warm hug. I was aware of more muscle in his arms and chest even from a brief embrace.

"You look fabulous, Lil. London agrees with you," he said, pulling out my chair.

"You're looking fit yourself." Maggie's comment came back to me.

"Thanks. Lots of free time equals lots of gym time."

"Sorry I'm late. Last minute conference call."

"No problem. It gave me time to study the menu," he said.

"I used to come to this place when I was over here. The food reminds me of visiting my grandmother. She made the best pierogies, filled with cheese and potato or sauerkraut. A great meal on a cold, wet day. Really sticks to your ribs."

"Well, you can order for me, then."

"What?"

"When I moved to Singapore, I promised myself that I'd try new things. Live, where I could, like a native. New foods, new culture. When in Rome, or in this case, when in London ..."

"Eat Polish?"

We both laughed.

"I'm at your mercy. Be gentle." His eyes twinkled as he grinned at me across the table.

This was fun. I'd never ordered for anyone else before.

"Okay. Let me see if they still have their sampler platter," I said, opening the menu. When the waitress came by I ordered food for the two of us, as well as wine for me and beer for Greg.

"So, tell me. How is life in the Far East? What have you been doing with yourself?"

"It's really different. Makes Toronto seem like a small town. So many people, all living and working in such a small space. People are friendly but the language is a barrier, although not so much where we live. The company found us a beautiful apartment in an area that's really the foreigners' ghetto. It's like a gated community. Everyone speaks English in addition to at least one other language but going outside the community, it's different."

Other than saying 'we' once, Greg hadn't mentioned Sophia yet.

Was I reading something into nothing?

"How is Simon?" he asked.

"He's ready to start fresh in Boston. The Manchester situation rocked his world. It's the first setback he's ever experienced on a professional level. I'm sure he saw himself as Chair of the Department or President of the University within five years. This new post is tenure-track and as soon as he tossed his hat into the ring, he was destined to make the short-list. He told me he likes Boston more than he imagined he would but would be happier if Jean-Marc were there, too, right now."

"It's tough."

"Getting settled in a new place?"

"No," Greg said. "Making a relationship work."

I didn't expect Sophia to be brought up this way. There was a pause while I debated probing further. I figured Greg was weighing the benefits of unloading on me at the same time. He reached a conclusion first.

"Do you think I'm a chauvinist?"

"A what?"

"Do you think I want a woman to be subservient? To be home instead of working? To make less than I do, so that I feel more like a man?"

"No. No. And a third no," I replied. "Where is this coming from?"

"From Sophia. Not in so many words, but ..."

The waitress came by with our food so our conversation stopped until she left.

"But what?"

"When she got the opportunity to go to Singapore, I supported her decision one hundred percent. I didn't balk or ask what I'd do. I understood it was a promotion. For three years, her career would take centre stage."

"What about that spousal appointment the company had lined up for you? The one you told me about before you left for Singapore?" I asked.

"Turned out it was just teaching one course at a local college. It ended after one year."

"So how have you been keeping busy?"

He chuckled. "This might make you laugh, but I figured it was the perfect time for me to finish my dissertation. Not for an academic position but for my own satisfaction, a sense of closure."

"And, is that what you've been doing?"

He shrugged. "That's how I started. She worked and I stayed home, ostensibly typing. But, being so far away, I lost motivation. For about six months I sat around the apartment, went downstairs to the gym to work out, read stuff. I was getting frustrated and Sophia was getting angry."

"Because you weren't doing much?"

"I don't know. She said she didn't like the fact I wasn't working on my dissertation. But she said it would be okay if I just wanted to relax, I just wasn't supposed to gripe about it."

I was confused and that must have registered on my face.

"She wanted me to just be happy to be there. With her," he said. "Even if I wasn't doing anything that I considered worthwhile. Being with her was supposed to be enough."

I couldn't believe what I was hearing. Greg was expressing a slightly different version of exactly the way I felt with Oliver.

"So we've been fighting lately," he continued. "Not screaming. More like not talking. Things will get better for a while then some little thing blows it up again."

"Have you tried counseling?"

He shrugged. "She's too busy."

"What if you went to see a counselor?"

"I don't know."

"Was it ever like this between you when you were in Toronto?"

He thought it over. "No. I don't think so. But we were both working then."

"So maybe it's just the pressure of living abroad. Two careers, one busier than the other right now."

He put down his utensils and looked at me. "I feel like she looks at me and sees a failure. Like I'm not what she bargained for."

"Every couple has their ups and downs. You're a great guy. An ass would have told her not to go to Singapore or to go alone. You're supportive, smart and the best guy a girl could ask for."

"You're sweet, Lil."

"But you've got to find something to do for yourself. How many hours do you figure it would take to finish your dissertation?"

"I don't know."

"Bullshit. Give me a range."

"Maybe forty or fifty."

"Okay. I'll be your coach. Each week, I'll check in with you to be sure you're making progress. It's not about a sprint to the finish. It's about being steady and consistent. Then you can send the bloody draft off to the committee, they can set a date and Dr. Greg Gallagher, here you come."

"Ah, Lil, you don't have to."

"I want to see you succeed. You were there for me."

He smiled. "I guess I am seeing a counselor."

"Oh, shut up and eat the rest of those pierogies before I steal them."

When the waitress passed by, I ordered two shot glasses of honey-flavoured vodka. As she poured them, Greg looked at me, puzzled.

"Vodka?"

"Don't question. Just drink." I raised my glass and looked at Greg. "Here's to the next time we meet up, with PhDs and more pierogies under our belts."

He laughed. "I'll drink to that!" And we did.

CHAPTER 24

EVERY WEEK THAT SPRING AND SUMMER, GREG DID EMAIL ME, sometimes with selections from chapters, sometimes with questions. I had never supervised a dissertation. It was strangely gratifying to see the work come together. Of course, I knew what it was like to be in Greg's shoes, particularly the importance of keeping up momentum. By September, all that was left for him to do was to crosscheck his footnotes against his running bibliography, to be sure all citations were accounted for and the formatting was correct, all housekeeping tasks for which he did not need my editorial eye.

The timing was perfect because in October I was asked to go down to Boston for six months to set up another office. This was fantastic. The challenge was intriguing and, once again, Simon and I could be neighbours. My employer took care of all the details; they found a nice furnished apartment close to the centre of Boston where the new office was located, and I flew down the Friday before Canadian Thanksgiving. They had the apartment stocked with food so that all I had to do was turn the key and I was home. The first person I rang was Simon.

"Welcome to America," he said.

"Thanks. You sound like a PR hack greeting the pilgrims."

"I'm simply being well-mannered. How was your flight?"

"Smooth as a knife through butter. Seemed like they'd just served drinks and it was over. How are you doing?"

"Fine."

"And Jean-Marc?"

"He's getting a bit stroppy. The paperwork isn't going as quickly as we'd hoped and he's not taking it well."

"I realize I'm not a sexy Parisian, and my culinary skills are definitely sub-par compared to his, but if you're brave and unattached on Monday, want to come over for Canadian Thanksgiving dinner?"

"Absolutely, but I wonder if there will be a turkey to be found. They're still fattening them up for November, El."

I sighed. "So many cultural nuances to learn."

"No matter. Any fowl will do. What may I bring as a housewarming gift? Have you had a chance to figure out what housekeeping necessity is missing?"

"Not yet. Just bring yourself. It's been far too long."

"Come, come, Lily. What kind of rube do you think I've become? Be warned, the default will be fresh flowers and alcohol."

"That's why you're such a good guest."

"Until Monday then, Madame Chef. Or, as Jean-Marc would say, *a bientot.*"

"Bring your appetite," I said and hung up.

Simon arrived that Monday just as I was basting the roast duck. He had offered to come by and help prepare dinner but I told him I'd rather have his help cleaning up. Truth was, I still hadn't a good sense of where everything was in the apartment. I didn't want to appear a total domestic wreck when I couldn't find a spatula or a baster.

Greeting him at the front door wearing an apron, I could barely see his face behind the enormous bouquet of fall flowers. His other hand clutched a large bottle of wine tied with a bow. I took the bouquet and was greeted by his sly grin.

"What's so funny?"

"This is such an unlikely picture," he said. "Lily Halton, homemaker."

"Do you want to go hungry?"

"Let me taste your culinary creations first then I shall answer that question."

I laughed.

"Why do you think I brought a large bottle of wine?" he asked as I beckoned him inside. He walked in and looked around. "Splendid digs. You've arrived."

"Thanks. Dinner should be ready in half an hour."

Being away from home, it was so nice to spend the holiday with Simon. I'd asked for the Monday to get settled before I started on the task of setting up the new office. We caught up over roast duck with root vegetables, salad, potatoes and homemade apple pie and talked about what I should see in my six months in Boston. Simon seemed equally pleased to have some company because it appeared as though Jean-Marc's arrival was delayed further still.

"What's the snag?" I asked. "His business or the paperwork?"

"Both. He thought he could leave the bistros but the fellow he'd been training went back to Paris to take care of a sick parent. And the paperwork is mired in bureaucratic purgatory."

"He can visit though, can't he?"

"He can, from the point of view of immigration, but he will not leave the bistros in the hands of just anyone so he won't visit, yet."

"So when are you going over?"

Simon scowled. "That, too, is up in the air. I'm toiling away trying to finish the edited volume before this two-year post ends. I want to be absolutely sure that no one on faculty could possibly resist keeping me on here and a major publication should assure that. Jean-Marc is not at all patient with me when I rush a visit or when my mind isn't totally focused on him, so better I finish here and then he and I can escape to Morocco or Spain for at least three weeks."

I clapped my hands. "So I have you all to myself for six months?"

"Only if you're gentle."

I crossed my heart. "Promise."

He raised one finger and wagged it back and forth. "Ah ah ah, missy! You forget that I know how like a martinet you can be," he said, clutching his belly.

I laughed as I looked at my watch. "I wondered how long it would take before you brought up that old chestnut."

"Charming and punctual. You see? I am irresistible!"

I raised my glass of wine. "To being irresistible."

"Oh, stop, you'll make me blush," he said as we clinked the crystal.

For the next six months, Simon and I spent part of every weekend together. It was the perfect antidote to my arduous work week and his publication schedule. I was determined not to make the same mistake I did during my Oxford postdoc. I worked hard but also wanted to see and experience Boston while I was there. Simon served as my companion and unofficial tour guide. We saw performances by the Boston Symphony Orchestra and Boston Lyric Opera, went to the Institute of Contemporary Art, BSA Space, Paul Revere House, the J.F. Kennedy Library, and he took me to visit the Widener Library at Harvard where he liked to work. Sometimes I got to set the agenda. One weekend we drove out to the Berkshires just to see the countryside. Being a hockey player, I managed to get two tickets to a Boston Bruins game and although he had no idea what was going on, Simon gamely came along, but he stopped short when I suggested we both try rowing on the Charles River.

When the Christmas holidays rolled around, neither of us had any place else to go so Simon decided to host a themed holiday dinner for the graduate students in his department who were not able to go home. In honour of his adopted homeland, the theme for the gift exchange was the American Revolution and everyone was encouraged to come as their favourite historical figure. This of course meant that we had five George Washingtons, three Paul Reveres and three Betsy Rosses. Simon, being the provocateur, was Benedict Arnold and insisted upon being called General Arnold all evening. I decided to go as Benjamin Franklin just to shake things up a bit. Once again, I took home what I suspected was Simon's gift for me – a red, white and blue vibrator with an electrical cord attached, tagged 'Benny's Best Friend'.

The spring went by faster than I imagined possible. I had managed to recruit three bright people, one woman and two men, to staff the new office, and we had already begun to make the necessary connections to make the office self-sustaining when I returned to Toronto later that spring.

Simon was absorbed by his edited volume. His motivation was strong. As soon as he finished and submitted it to the publisher, he could, without guilt, fly over to see Jean-Marc. I had just finished a meeting with three genomics researchers one Monday morning when Simon called.

"Finished?" I asked.

"Are you psychic, El?" His voice was uncharacteristically flat.

"Congratulations. When do you fly off to see Jean-Marc?"

"Sooner than I had anticipated, but not for the right reasons."

"What are you talking about, Simon?"

There was a moment's silence. "It's over."

"With Jean-Marc?"

"No. Harvard. My position is not being renewed."

"What?" I could not believe it. "How?"

"I don't know. Talking with colleagues at conferences, they warned me that this particular tenure track position has become a tenured position only once. I, of course, thought they were either exaggerating or that the university had not yet seen someone of my exemplary quality."

"Oh, Simon."

"But it seems that I grossly overestimated my intellectual seductive lure or I underestimated the institution's agenda."

"Do they know about the edited volume?"

"The Chair even mentioned it as he told me my position was not to be renewed."

"So what now?"

"I don't know, El," Simon said. "I really don't know."

"Have you told Jean-Marc?"

"Not yet. I don't know what to say. First Manchester, now this? What ..." His voice trailed off. I had never heard such despair in him and it frightened me.

"Meet me at my place. After ..."

"Work? Which I have until end of term? No, Lily. I'm going home now."

"To do what?"

"To have a drink. To sleep. To regroup." He hung up.

I remember feeling gutted with each FOAD letter that slipped through my mail slot but I had never lost a job. I chose to leave.

And I had other options. I debated going over to Simon's place to be sure he was fine but then thought he might want a bit of time to mourn the latest lost future. If he was still holed up in his apartment this time tomorrow, I'd camp outside his door until he let me in. I knew from experience that sitting home alone, stewing and getting depressed, didn't lead to anything productive.

When I got home there were two emails waiting for me. Simon wrote saying I wasn't to worry. After the initial shock wore off, he was already combing H-Net and jobs.ac.uk for openings. He fundamentally believed that academia wanted and needed him and that this was an anomalous glitch.

The other email was from Greg. It was short, sweet and a complete shocker: "Good news, bad news. Good news, defense date set for 30 April in Toronto. Bad news, Sophia and I split up. So I'll be staying in Toronto after my exam."

CHAPTER 25

OVER THE COURSE OF TWO WEEKS THAT APRIL, ALL THREE OF US were reunited in Toronto. I was, however, the only one who was there by choice. The challenge of setting up the Boston office was exactly what I needed professionally and it renewed in me a sense that I had made the right decision to return to the communications field. When I got back to the Toronto office, my supervisor not only congratulated me on a job well done, but she also gave me a substantial raise. It looked like buying my own place could happen sooner than I had anticipated.

Simon had finished his formal duties at Harvard and was uncomfortable hanging about where he was, in his words, "neither appreciated nor intellectually welcome". His relationship with Jean-Marc was increasingly strained – Simon wanted Jean-Marc to shift his plans and to come to live in Toronto but Jean-Marc said with no firm position, it was just too much of a risk. Simon didn't help matters by giving ultimatums. He was looking for posts but at this late date, many searches were well underway and there were fewer opportunities available. He was so unnerved by the latest setback that he had not done a thing to find lodging. He was usually so organized. I had never before seen this side of Simon but I was sure it would pass. I offered my spare bedroom for as long as it took for him to find a place.

Greg came back to Toronto and spent the week before his oral exam at his parents' home, reviewing his notes. His goals, he said, were to finish his PhD, find a place to live, look for work and then figure out next steps.

Simon was languishing in as dark a place as I'd ever seen him and so I broached the topic of celebrating with Greg gingerly one evening.

"I was thinking that we three should get together to celebrate Greg getting his PhD. What do you think?"

Simon shrugged. "Sure, but there's no guarantee everything will have gone well so a celebration might be in poor taste."

I understood what he was getting at. "I know. He might have tons of revisions to do, but at least he'll know exactly what to do for those last steps."

"If he can trust them."

"Who?"

"His committee. I've grown suspicious of all promises made by those who dwell in ivory towers."

"Simon, I agree that you've had a couple of bad experiences, but you can't ..."

"Generalize? Draw conclusions? Precisely what phrase do you think appropriate, El?"

"Look, you're getting ahead of yourself. Greg just wants to finish. To get the degree. I don't think he's looking to spend a career in academia."

"Exceedingly wise."

"We're his friends and we should support him."

"Valid point."

"It's been years and there's no one at the Institute who'll know him now," I said. "So there's no big party to be had. I was thinking of the three of us going for dinner."

Simon was silent.

"Come on, Simon. It won't be same without you. At last, we're all back in the same place."

"And miraculously no one's in hospital," he said.

"Right."

"Fine. You're absolutely right, Lily. He deserves to have the achievement celebrated, if not the original decision."

Since arriving from Boston, his self-confidence had plummeted and he had become more pessimistic about his own future. But I was damned if I was going to let Simon sulk all night. "Come on, Mr. Smarty Pants. Would you really have me believe that you regret finishing your PhD? What would Simon Beale have become otherwise? An investment banker? A party planner? An accountant?"

I had intended my questions to yield a smile. Instead, he looked stricken as he contemplated a serious reply. No quips. No witty retort. Just the muttered statement, "I have no idea."

One week later, Simon and I met Greg for dinner at The Roof Lounge of the Park Hyatt Hotel across from the ROM. I thought the view would serve as a metaphor for our new horizons and I'd always loved the treat of going there for drinks as a graduate student; it reminded me that although a student, I was an adult who liked a little sophistication now and then.

Greg wore a tailored dark suit and a crisp white shirt to the examination. I couldn't remember ever seeing him this dressed up, other than at his wedding, and he looked even more handsome. Simon, although still in a bit of a funk, displayed none of that outside the apartment and was resplendent in sport coat and light trousers, lavender waistcoat, white shirt and a silk bow tie. In honour of the once-in-a-lifetime nature of the evening, I wore a little black dress and heels and was forced to endure much good-natured ribbing from both men.

Greg whistled as I walked to greet him in the lobby of the hotel. "Well, who knew?" he joked.

"Who indeed. Methinks the lady doth have shapely legs," Simon said.

I rolled my eyes. "Must I ask for the kiddie table when we go upstairs?"

"Oh, I assure you, we're not thinking kiddie-type thoughts," Greg said.

"Perhaps you should book a room," Simon said, gesturing to the hotel front desk with a flick of his head.

"No, I can muster self-control. I am almost a doctor, too, you know," Greg said.

Simon and I congratulated him at the same time.

"Well done. And their final verdict?" Simon asked.

"Minor corrections," Greg replied.

"That's terrific," I said.

"Thanks, Lil. Your coaching and editing helped a lot."

"It was nothing," I said.

"Shall we move this meeting of the mutual admiration society upstairs?" Simon asked. "I believe that a bottle of champagne would make a fine fourth for our group."

We all walked to the elevators and went up to the eighteenth floor.

That evening was an oasis. Simon, for once, forgot that he had no post. Greg didn't mention his separation or his job hunt and I didn't talk about being single. We celebrated being together, with drinks flowing and good food, literally on top of the world. I looked at both of them and smiled, thinking of everything we'd been through together and wondering how long it would be before forces beyond our control, such as jobs or partners or life, would pull us apart again. I took a deep breath and sighed as I tried to take it all in, to live in the moment. Greg noticed.

"Why the heavy breathing, Lil? You growing tired of us already?"

"No. It's been so long since all of us were together and I just wondered how long this will last."

"It depends," Greg said. "How long do we want it to last?"

"You give us great powers," Simon said, shaking his head slowly. "If there is no work to be had here, will one of you keep me in the style to which I've grown accustomed?"

"Don't you mean you and Jean-Marc?" Greg asked.

"You do know how to cut to the quick," Simon said.

"Oh, don't tell me …," Greg said.

Simon pursed his lips. "It would appear that all three of us will be single by morning."

"What happened?" Greg asked before turning to me. "Lily, you didn't say anything."

"I'm hearing this for the first time myself. Simon?"

"Jean-Marc says he can't take the dual strain of distance and uncertainty about my finding a new post. I could work anywhere in the English-speaking world but when is a mystery. He's breaking up with me. He says I'm not ready to settle down."

"So go back to Manchester to be with him," Greg said.

"And do what all day? His laundry? My nails? I need to find an academic post."

"If you love him, find any kind of work," Greg said.

"A noble idea but utterly impractical for me. Unlike you and Lily, I am only trained for the academic life. I don't do anything else. I can't teach high school without going back to teachers' college. I have no other work experience. Even if I were willing to get other work, I'm sure as soon as I tell them I've got a PhD, they will ignore me because I'm overqualified in their eyes. They could care less about Newton, about degrees or academic awards. No, it's got to be an academic position or I'm doomed."

I shook my head. "Hey, hey, hey, this celebration has taken an ugly turn. Yes, Simon's in a shitty place right now, both personally and professionally. Greg, you're staring divorce in the face and you're unemployed and living with your parents, so that may top Simon's current crappy circumstances. I'm almost forty, with a good job, but a career that's my second choice and I sleep alone every night. So we're three adults whose lives look worse at this point that we'd imagined ten years ago. But we're healthy and tomorrow we'll start to work toward something better. We still have choices."

"Such as what, Little Miss Sunshine?" Simon asked.

I gestured to the outdoor balcony. "We can choose to walk out on that ledge and jump," I said. "Or we can raise another glass to a better future? Are you drinking with me or jumping?"

The boys looked at each other.

"Ah, Lily, trust you to put it all in perspective. I, for one, choose not to end it all tonight, so ...," said Simon, raising his glass.

"Okay," said Greg. "I'll succumb to peer pressure," and he raised his glass, too.

"To the three of us. Reunited, overeducated, and friends always!"

It was no surprise that we closed the place that night. None of us had anything specific to go home to and it had been years since we'd just sat around chatting. When the lounge closed we all walked down Bloor Street to Philosophers' Walk, south past the ROM and the Music Faculty, down to Hoskin Avenue. We sat on the stone wall surrounding Trinity College and continued talking. At one point, I wondered if we were going to pull an all-nighter but Greg had a morning meeting with a lawyer to go over a separation agreement and he left Simon and me to hail a cab out to his parents around two-thirty in the morning. I asked Simon if he wanted to walk or take a taxi back to the condo. He wasn't ready to go home so we walked, in silence, along the edge of the Back Campus, through the Hart House archway, across King's College Circle. Just in front of Convocation Hall, I decided I would broach the topic of Jean-Marc.

"Simon, I'm sorry about you and Jean-Marc. I mean, about the break-up."

He shrugged and sat down. "*Ç'est la vie.* Or as Piaf sang, '*Je ne regrette rien.*'"

I sat down on the steps beside him. "You're taking it ... I don't know what to say. Really well? Philosophically?"

Simon stopped. "How else can I take it? Neither of us is prepared to deny who we are, what we are. Bloody circumstances got in the way."

"But if you really ..."

"If I what? If I really wanted him? If I was really in love?"

"I didn't mean to say that you weren't in love," I said.

"I adore him. Living apart from him these past two years nearly ate me alive. But I threw myself into my work. I thought I was laying down the groundwork so we could be together for the rest of our lives." He laughed. "You know what came in the post yesterday? They forwarded his papers for his green card. He can work in the US and now I can't work there."

"I'm so sorry." I threw my arms around him and hugged him.

"Oh, Lily. This is not how I planned it."

I stroked his hair. "I know."

"The beating... that hurt, but not half as much as this."

"I know."

"What's become of my life? What the hell am I supposed to do?" he asked, his face buried in my hair. Before I could say anything, I felt something moist against my neck. Simon was sobbing and all I could do was hold him.

That summer was a strange one. My work was going well and I was still exploring the on-line dating sites for fun. Greg had moved out of his parents' home, found a managerial position back at the plant, and was working through his separation from Sophia. But Simon was in limbo. He was still staying with me. Some days, when I came home from work, he would be full of enthusiasm, telling me about the latest round of opportunities posted online or the progress he was making on the edited volume. That was the Simon I knew. Other days, he wouldn't even shave or dress, spending hours sequestered alone in his room, emerging only to refill his coffee mug and give a cursory greeting. This side of Simon was new to me.

When I thought about it, I'd behaved much the same way the year I spent at loose ends before going off to Oxford. That year was difficult for me because I was impatient to start my new career and I had expected everything to fall into place. I imagined for Simon it was even more difficult. He was not only my intellectual superior, but he had spent time at two of the world's leading universities and now would have to somehow explain the interruption on his CV. He had, in his words, "fallen from a greater height." As much as budget cuts and university politics were beyond any single person's control, I knew Simon believed that excellence was rewarded. I also think that this was the first time that Simon had ever had to face a professional setback; he had never had to learn to adjust his expectations or goals.

Breaking up with Jean-Marc didn't help matters. I wondered if Simon would rebound by taking a series of lovers. Instead, he withdrew from all contact other than with me and Greg.

As I did when Simon was in hospital in Oxford, I would ring Greg when Simon was in one of his emotional troughs. I wanted to be sure that I was doing everything possible to see him through this rough patch.

"Lil, don't worry," Greg said over coffee at the local café.

"He's fine for a week or two then he goes to the dark place."

"He's just recalibrating."

"I hope so."

He paused. "You survived."

I knew what he was talking about. "Yeah, I guess."

"And, if I remember rightly, it took about a year."

I nodded, hoping he wouldn't bring up our one and only sexual encounter and the uncomfortable aftermath. "Getting the postdoc pulled me out of my funk."

"And I'm sure when Simon gets the next interview he'll be back to his old self."

I decided to change the subject. "How is the new job? And your new place?"

"The job is terrific. It's a new position, working with the team on market evaluations for new designs. There are opportunities to travel but I'll be based in Toronto."

"What are they working on?"

"Green cars. Confidential stuff. If I tell you any more, I'll have to kill you," he said smiling.

I raised my hand. "I heard nothing."

"Good plan. My new place is working out pretty well. I have to say it feels weird, starting from scratch again."

"Yeah. Six months from now, you'll forget all about the blip."

He shook his head. "Ever weirder to think of my marriage as a blip."

"Sorry. I didn't mean for it to come out like that."

"I know, Lil. I never thought that I'd be almost forty before I finished my degree, just starting my career and working on a divorce."

"I had a different vision, too."

"At least you've had a few years to lay down the groundwork. And you're not divorcing."

"Is that worse than being single?"

"Being single can be a choice."

"So is divorcing. Are you sure you and Sophia can't work things out?" The moment I said the words I wanted to reach out and stuff them back in my throat.

Greg sat there, thinking. "I've turned it over in my mind a thousand times. We want different things. She's wants the best of everything. Nice cars, jewelry, designer clothes and shoes, exotic vacations. She could afford a lot of that on her own, but then what was I supposed to do? I'm not cut out to be a house husband. I need to be of use. To do something. If I stayed, I'd have lots of nice stuff but lose my self-respect, as a man, as a person. I'd be miserable and life's too short to be miserable."

"I'm sorry."

"I am, too. She's not evil. We're just too different."

We sat there for a moment. "Life is funny, eh, Greg? It all seemed so simple when we were in our twenties."

"Yeah. When did it become so complicated?"

"Around thirty-five for me. Just after I finished."

"Everything still seemed possible then," he said.

I nodded.

A few days later Simon was bouncing off the walls. He had received an email from a university in Glasgow inviting him to interview for a position that would begin in January. He had also been offered a single elective half-course in the fall in Toronto, albeit at the last minute because the other person had been offered a full-time post.

"I am a man reborn," he said over dinner one evening.

"Hallelujah!" I said.

"I sense that you share my glee?"

"You haven't been … um, your usual *bon vivant* self lately."

He bowed his head and placed one hand over his heart. "*Mea culpa, mea culpa*. I shall never be able to repay your kindnesses. You have enduring patience, Lily. I look forward to sharing my future successes with you."

"When do you go?"

"In three weeks. The interview's booked for August 27."

"Do you have to give a lecture to a class or just a job talk to the committee?"

"A job talk, a luncheon with all the candidates, and then the interview."

I was puzzled. "A lunch with the rest of the people going up for the position? That's bizarre."

"I agree."

"So that's not just the way things are done over there?"

"Not in my experience. It's usually more like a French farce. One candidate being hustled into a room milliseconds before another candidate is brought into the same room. Doors opening and closing, one after another. I do pledge to restrain myself when I am among the other candidates and not to shine too brightly."

"Ah, Simon the Modest is back."

"Indeed, he is."

I smiled. "Hmmm, I don't know which Simon I prefer, now that I'm reminded of your alter ego. Or should I say your substantial ego?"

"Lily, dearest. When I've secured this post, I shall give you the greatest gift one friend can bestow upon another."

"What's that?"

"I shall move out."

I laughed. "Well, take this in the spirit in which it's meant. I look forward to that."

"Then, if you'll excuse me, I have a great deal of work to do to prepare. My talk is ready but I'd like to tell them that the edits on the volume are complete and that I can begin my next project." With that he cleared his dishes and went off to his room.

For the next three weeks, Simon worked day and night, with the excitement of a child and the drive of an Olympian. When we parted at the airport, he was brimming with his usual self-confidence. It was so good to have Simon back.

———•●•———

The trip was a brief one. Simon flew out, stayed two days and then flew back to Toronto to prepare his course notes for the fall term. Greg and I went out to meet him at the airport in a show of support and solidarity. When we got back to my condo, I peppered Simon with questions.

"Were they impressed with your talk?"

"They seemed so."

"And the luncheon? Was it weird to be sitting with the other candidates?"

"It was actually the first indication I had that I must be the front-running candidate. I was the most senior by far of the four of us. Two of the others were still completing their degrees and the other woman had been out just one year."

"What about the interview?" I asked.

"That went well, although the Chair opened with the most ignorant query. He looked me straight in the eye and asked, 'Why have you not been able to keep your previous posts?' He obviously had not noticed the recent budget cuts in Britain or the revolving turnstile nature of some key two-year 'tenure-track' appointments."

"What did you say then?"

"I told him my penchant for brilliance and buggery might be putting off some of the less accomplished scholars!"

"Oh Simon, you didn't …," I said, laughing along with Greg.

"That's sticking it to him, as it were," said Greg.

"There is a coda," Simon said.

"What?" I asked.

"They asked the textbook question regarding my short, medium and long-term research plans. When I listed the three monographs, two edited volumes, five articles and new research I had planned or already underway, one of the committee members actually murmured aloud, 'If he does all that, he'll make us look bad.'"

"Are they for real? Do you really want to work there?" asked Greg.

"Sounds like you'll be buying kilts and haggis soon," I said.

Simon chuckled. "I do have the legs for a kilt but not the stomach for haggis."

He truly believed the post was his to lose. So he was flabbergasted when, two days later, he received an email saying that they had selected one of the other candidates.

CHAPTER 26

At first, Simon seemed fine. He was disappointed, to be sure, so he channeled all his energy into lectures for his contract half-course. He endured the humiliation of not being entrusted with the photocopy code or a phone because he was, in the words of the departmental secretary, "merely a sessional instructor". It mattered little to her that in Manchester he had headed up an entire institute or that he was an award-winning researcher. He described his office as a contract kiddie corral, with four bare desks shared by all the sessionals; there were no computers, printers, or telephones provided so he went in to the office only for his formal office hours.

He resigned himself to making a few thousand dollars that fall and resuming his job search. If I had been meticulous when I had been searching for an academic post, he was flawlessly thorough, applying for everything from postdocs to limited term appointments to tenure track positions, even Associate Professorships. His logic was to cast a wide net to land a job as quickly as possible.

"With a post in hand, it's that much easier to move one's career along," he told me over dinner in early December.

"That's true in industry as well," I said. "They say it's best not to leave a job before you've secured your next job."

"It is lovely to contemplate a world where that is an option."

"Simon, something's got to break soon."

"Other than my resolve?"

I smiled. "I meant you've got to catch a break soon."

"Why? Your hunt yielded nothing."

"Don't remind me."

"Doesn't it irk you?"

"Of course it does," I said. "Every bloody day but I'd be a full-fledged idiot if I didn't recognize the fact that two or three years out, with no interviews, I was a dead fish in the huge pool of applicants."

"I feel exactly the same."

"But you've had two stellar positions. The award, the publications, the research and management experience to set up a unit. That has to count for something," I said.

"One hopes. On the other hand, you had a previous career that you could return to with little difficulty."

"True. That's what kept me sane. It took the sting out of my failure."

"I have no such occupational safety net, El."

"You could retrain."

"As what?"

I paused for a moment. "Would you consider teaching high school?"

He pursed his lips. "That's risky. If I graduate at a time when there is a surplus of teachers, I'll be no further ahead in any sphere but student debt."

"Point taken. Any other interests?"

"Intelligent, gorgeous men."

I laughed. "Be serious. You drive, don't you?"

"Being a cabbie is out of the question," he said.

"What about a career in insurance?"

Simon glared at me.

"There should be some sort of course or workshop for how to turn the skills we polished doing the PhD into jobs outside the academy," I said and shrugged. "I think the system is flawed. If I were the only one who didn't land an academic job, that would have been hard to accept but my tough luck, but I was reading an article just the other day. It said three-quarters of faculty in the US today are working as adjuncts. Those posts can evaporate on a dime."

"I read the most dismal statistic yesterday. Only three percent of arts PhDs are getting full-time posts in the current market," Simon said. "What is everyone else doing?"

"Last week, I met a guy who graduated with his PhD in American history, same year as me, with a wife and daughter; he was installing bathrooms to pay the rent and keeping up his academic society memberships on the off chance that one day he'd get lucky."

"I wish I had more saleable skills than translating Latin."

"Where did we go wrong? How could we have missed this?"

Simon just shrugged. It wasn't like him to be without a quick retort.

"I wish we'd all finished science PhDs," I said. "Read the job boards. Posts in quantum physics and genomics are everywhere."

"One doesn't choose an area of study for a PhD based on potential employment."

"Too bad, eh?"

"That's ludicrous. What about passion? Aptitude? Ability? Even lack of ability as a factor?"

I wanted to lighten the mood. "I'm sure if anyone could switch from arts to sciences you could, Simon. You are the genius among us."

"It's too late to start again." He sighed. "I feel like we're at a wake, El."

"It felt like that when I finally gave up. I was mourning the death of my goal. That was tough. You know me, Simon, I'm a stubborn old biddy and I hate to admit defeat but I couldn't deny the numbers. Every post gets hundreds of applications and it turns out that experience and publications can actually hinder an application. No one tells you that in grad school. Crafty department Chairs save on salaries by picking the least experienced candidates if they're hiring tenure track. They can save even more by hiring ..."

"Don't say it. People like me. Contract employees."

"I remember what that was like, Simon."

"I'd never thought that my employment situation would be so tenuous."

"I couldn't take it after a few years so I buried the dream."

Simon chuckled. "There should be a specific requiem for all those whose dreams of a life spent in academe are quashed."

I smiled. "Yeah. Something dirge-like, with suitable gravitas. What do you think?"

"Allusions to that medieval poem, *Gaudeamus*," Simon said.

"Yeah. They should do another set of verses to warn new graduates. They can sing it as they convocate."

"Include a bit of mock Latin, perhaps?"

"Perfect."

He stood up and began to sing, "*Gaudeamus igitur, Iuvenes dum sumus.*"

I joined in for the repeat, improvising new lines.

"Aging, broke *graduati*, No one wants your PhD!"

Simon continued with the next line, "*Post iucundam iuventutem ...*"

I paused for a second, smiled and sang the line back with parodied lyrics. "Posts are contract *servitudem*," I sang.

Simon continued, "*Post molestam senectutem ...*"

"Temp posts pay shit, can't buy food-em!"

Simon groaned. "We can do better, El. How about, 'We complain and they say, 'Screw 'em'!'"

I laughed as I thought over the last few lines of the stanza.

"You're fucked over by the system," I sang.

Simon held up one finger as he translated my line and finished the repeat with, "*Futui super ipsum systema.*"

We both howled with laughter.

"A bit rough round the edges but methinks we've got something here, El."

"Yeah, but can we parlay it into remunerative work?"

"With all that Latin it's a niche market at best."

"Keep the faith, Simon. Keep the faith."

There was still a glimmer of hope.

So long as he had some form of association with a university, Simon seemed to be holding it together, but when his course ended and after the distraction of the holidays passed, the rest of the winter stretched out before him like a barren landscape devoid of any form of life. His descent was gradual. As the thin letters of rejection began to arrive, he slipped further into depression. The first few he opened. After a while, I noticed envelopes tossed among the newspapers and magazines, in the bathroom, used as coasters on the coffee table, all unopened.

More often than not, I'd come home from work to find Simon asleep in his room. By the spring, it was obvious that he was drinking to dull his pain. When we lived in Oxford, Simon drank but never to excess. I never saw him slurring his words or vomiting behind the pub. He paced himself. Even now, he would drink during the day so that when I came home, he'd be sleeping it off. On weekends, when I was home, he'd lie in bed until close to noon and then read most of the rest of the day.

He was crafty and I never found bottles under his bed or hidden in his closet. It was difficult to search for clues in any case because he almost never left the condo and I was away at work during the week. I tried to talk to him, to encourage him to get help, but he deftly rebuffed my attempts. There were days when he seemed to be getting better, climbing out of the hole. Then he would relapse.

When he was up he would often clean. One day, I was gathering all the garbage to take down the hall to the chute and in one bin I found a letter from the university where he had taught the last course the previous fall. Normally I wouldn't have read his mail but I was looking for any clue as to how to help him. The letter was an announcement of appointments for the latest round of courses and there was a note attached.

"Simon, sorry to say there's nothing for you this 'round. As you can see, all appointments went to instructors with more seniority. Maybe next year. Best of luck." The note was signed by the department chair. I crumpled the sheet and stuffed it into the garbage bag.

I couldn't spend the summer watching Simon waste away. I enlisted Greg's help in convincing him to see a counselor. Surprisingly, Simon agreed. He went twice a week throughout the summer and being able to vent to an impartial third-party seemed to make a difference. He eased back on the drinking and was sleeping more normally. When he got an invitation to speak to the new group of graduate students at the Institute he agreed immediately. He was keen to get back into a university setting, even for just an afternoon. It really was as if taking him out of the academy was like taking a fish out of water. He suggested to the department chair that I come to speak, too.

"We represent two different forms of graduates with different career trajectories," he said.

"I guess."

"You must come, El," Simon said. "To share your wisdom and to keep me from ranting. The way things are going I could discourage generations of graduate students."

"Okay. I'll go."

That afternoon Simon was sober, shaved and as close to the old Simon as I'd seen lately. We were two of five graduates and the eldest of the lot. Only one alumna had an academic job and that was an American who went back to the US to teach on a five-year contract at a small Midwestern college. She had signed her contract two months before her oral examination.

The incoming group of students looked so young. There were also students from each of the subsequent years so it ranged from new MA students to those finishing their PhDs. Some of the faculty members were there, too, although there had been considerable turnover since we had studied there. MacPhee was still hanging on to a post since mandatory retirement had been abolished some years back.

As I watched Simon being both honest and encouraging, it struck me that he had a knack for mentoring. It made me angry that his skills were being wasted by a system that had too few jobs and that didn't acknowledge real talent. When one student asked Simon if he would, knowing the career challenges, do his PhD in the same field, Simon replied, "Unequivocally, yes. We all have many skills and passions and this is what I was born to do. I could, without a doubt, be a passable clothing designer or raconteur-for-rent, a gigolo in other circles." He paused as some students giggled. "But teaching, researching and disseminating fascinating, illuminating analyses on topics that I adore is what I do best. If you feel the same way, so should you."

I was far more pragmatic in my responses, warning against going into debt for a degree that had a small chance of yielding employment and encouraging everyone to have a Plan B in place in case no academic job was forthcoming after two or three years. "I'm not saying anything that the magazines, newspapers and blogs haven't been saying for ages. Grad school is great, but like a blind date, don't have high expectations for a long-term relationship with the academy. You can lose a lot of years waiting for a full-time post that never comes."

Afterwards, there was a wine and cheese reception. Simon was besieged by students asking about his experiences in England and Boston. He was in his element as advisor. I kept an eye on what he was drinking but it seemed so long as he was chatting, the alcohol was in check.

As I turned my head, MacPhee had sidled up to me.

"So you've been wooed back to the corporate world, Lily?" he asked.

"More like driven back. There were no jobs to be found."

He shook his head. "I always thought you might have some challenges. Getting a post, I mean. There's a risk in choosing a non-traditional topic."

I wanted to spit in his drink. "Film *has* been around for more than a century."

"Yes, but as a medium for history of science or medicine? Where does that fit in? Which department will hire you? The history department believes you belong in Film Studies and Film Studies says apply to the history department." He sighed. "That was your major problem."

Before I could stop myself I blurted out, "So tell me, what is keeping Simon Beale, who is brilliant, from landing a position like yours?"

"You mean a tenured post?" MacPhee asked.

"Exactly."

MacPhee looked over at Simon and shrugged. "At this point, he's too old academically. My guess is, although his work is excellent, it's been so long since he graduated, and he's had too many short-term posts, that he'd be viewed as an expensive, high-risk prospect."

"He wasn't fired from those posts."

MacPhee shrugged. "Bottom line is he couldn't keep a job, couldn't play the political game." He downed the last of his wine. "All I can say is that I'm very glad I'm not young and just starting out." He laughed. "Don't know that I could land a job today."

I nodded.

"You'll be fine. Must be quite the discovery for your colleagues to learn you've got a PhD. Best of luck." He walked away. Good thing, because otherwise I might have done something I would have regretted.

Simon walked over. "Sharing words of wisdom with your supervisor, El?"

"What's that word? Bollocks."

"You never did have the patience to deal with prats or academic politics."

"Nope. I don't."

"Shall we go?" He flicked his college scarf over his shoulder. "I believe I've imparted everything I have to give."

"Yeah, I've had it. Let's get out of here."

"The cruel finger of irony. It seems only yesterday you were dying to get in here."

After the workshop, I convinced Simon to see another counselor, a job placement counselor. Simon went, reluctantly, and when he came home that evening was as deflated as ever I'd seen him. The counselor had been frank. With little job experience outside the academy, Simon would have to start almost at the bottom. He warned that many employers would be intimidated by Simon's PhD or not be able to see transferable skills. At thirty-six, he was encouraged to look at getting a college certificate, perhaps as a book editor or grant writer. The job hunt would be a long one. The counselor advocated patience and re-branding. Simon was brilliant but I didn't know if he had those particular skills.

CHAPTER 27

By the end of September, Simon was desperate. Like a drowning man, he clutched at the hope of getting at least one half course as his last vestige of true paedagogy, somewhere where his research and training would be appreciated. This time there was nothing for him. I encouraged him to apply for other research posts. He was a renowned scholar in his own field and doing research for another scholar was a step down, but he had to support himself. But when he inquired, he was told departments were obliged to give research assistantships to their own graduate students. When he looked into editing grant applications, he learned his name could be added to a list for six weeks of seasonal contract work available for a maximum of ten hours per week at the MA student rate. He couldn't survive on that.

I pushed him to look outside the university sphere. Speaking with a recruiter that I knew, Simon was advised to take his PhD off his resume because employers either didn't understand why someone with a doctorate would want to seek work outside the academy or they were intimidated by someone with more education. This was the second person who intimated the PhD was a resumé liability and Simon was furious. He said it was deceitful and disrespectful, to both potential employers and himself. "I can't turn off what I've learned and who I am just because I strike my education from the record," he said.

By mid-October, he was even more withdrawn. Pleas to go out, to talk, were politely deflected due to the course he was working on. I didn't know if he was still applying to other posts but if so, he kept that to himself. I felt helpless.

My cell phone rang while I was in the bathroom. The bloody thing kicks over to voicemail after just four rings and I was waiting for a call from a head-hunter so I bolted up off the seat. Pulling up my underwear, I almost fell flat on my face, tripping over my jeans, which were still unzipped and hanging around my ankles as I lurched toward my desk. I flipped open the phone as it was on the fourth ring before I'd even had a chance to check who was calling.

"Lily Halton here," I said, catching my breath to try to sound professional.

"Shit, Lil. Holy shit! Go online. This is unbelievable."

"Greg, I'll do it later," I said, struggling to pull up my pants one-handed. "I'm waiting for an important call."

"Now!"

It wasn't like him to be so insistent. "What is so damned ..."

"Take me with you!"

"What?"

"Take your damned phone with you. It's bad."

"What the hell are you babbling about?"

He drew a heavy breath. "Are you sitting at your computer?"

"I am now."

"Log on to YouTube."

"You want to me to ..."

"Just do it!" he said. "And put me on speaker phone beside you."

"Jesus, you're the king of drama today." I pressed the speaker phone button then tapped the keys as instructed. "Okay. I've got YouTube on screen."

Greg spoke the next words slowly and carefully. "Now, type 'PhD on fire, Toronto.'"

"Don't you have anything better to do than chase down the latest funny clip on flipping YouTube?"

"Lil, it's not funny."

"All right already."

I waited for my internet connection. I typed in the search term, the clip came up and I hit play. I immediately recognized Simon, standing in the middle of the campus lawn. It was a warm fall afternoon, the leaves were a riot of colour, and he was surrounded by a large circle of books, piled five or six high. He spoke directly into the camera as students crossed the lawn behind him.

"My name is Dr. Simon Beale. And this," he gestured with outstretched arms, "is my *alma mater*. I enrolled in the doctoral program here fourteen years ago. It was a fascinating experience, allowing me to delve into the erudite – and not so erudite – works of many scholars, absorbing new ideas, refuting others, while I honed my analytic skills. I also ate far too much fast food, drank far too little good whisky, and spent too much on substandard lodging. But graduate school is not about living the high life. I chose to relinquish the trappings of riches. I could have studied law or engineering."

He moved closer to the camera as if he was confiding a secret. "No. I chose, instead, to heed the siren's call of historical research and the solitary world of dusty, archives, research libraries and esoteric questions. I spent every waking moment of those graduate years in the company of these," and he bent down to pick up one of the books. "Fascinating seductive tomes. The doctorate promised training for a lifetime of epistemological challenges and was the ticket to moving up, from the rank of student to professor."

He slipped the book into the exact spot in the pile from which he'd taken it as if he were shelving it in a library. "But that promise is bullshit! The system, to which we have all ascribed, is broken. My *alma mater,* like all of them, is a lying, conniving *matris futuor*."

He turned to address some of the young students who had stopped to listen. "For those of you who are not Classics scholars, that is Latin for 'mother fucker'. Enroll in the program, pay the fees. Then you're robed, hooded, and booted out and, lo and behold, there is no permanent post to be had. Oh, there is a course to teach here and perhaps another there. You've become an itinerant academic. But live in Toronto on six and a half thousand dollars a year?"

Now he was walking around the inside of the circle, speaking directly to his live audience. "But each one of us believes that is just the fate of the dullards in the group. Poor deluded souls. Do everything right, publish articles, even a book, get teaching experience, and what have you done?"

He laughed. "You've merely assured yourself that you'll never get full-time work because you've priced yourself out of the market. There are at least fifty new graduates coming up behind you every year, and because they've done nothing yet, they're a cracking good cheap hire."

He made his way back to the centre of the circle. "I'm not alone in this. I have friends," and here he looked straight at the camera, "dear friends, who are in the same boat. Some gave up on their dream.

Thousands of others are also struggling. Many are mired in debt. We've put our lives on hold because maybe *this* year will be *the* year. We can't get real work in the universities because the universities are using contract positions as a form of intellectual scab labour. If we do get positions, they can be cut without warning if the winds of funding shift. Whole departments wiped out and faculty cut loose. Our lofty educations also keep us out of jobs outside the ivory tower. We are deemed overeducated, overqualified and intimidating."

He paused for a moment. "But I'm not feeling sorry for myself. I've decided to seize control," and he pointed round the circle of books. "I've built my own citadel, my own tower, and today I shall truly be master of my own destiny."

With that he left the frame and returned with two canisters, the liquid contents of which he began to pour carefully onto the books. "I've written to university presidents. But no one is listening. Our higher education system is broken. We're luring thousands of 'the best and the brightest' then refusing them entry to the very tower that they were once good enough to enter. Well, I refuse to spend one more day being less than I am."

He gently placed one canister behind him and looked straight into the video lens, pushing that errant lock of hair from his eyes. "I apologize to those of you who may find this difficult."

The books now soaked, he turned the canister over and doused his clothes. "I was never really one for all this social media stuff. But, as McLuhan said, 'The medium is ...' You know the rest."

His wet clothes clinging to his lean frame, he dropped the last canister. "Universities of the world, you cannot ignore what you're doing. Consider yourselves on notice."

He paused for a moment before he took a box of matches from his jeans pocket, and lit one. He walked over to the books, and slowly made a complete circuit, singing a stanza from *Gaudeamaus igitur* as the books slowly ignited, one by one:

> Vita nostra brevis est,
> Brevi finietur;
> Vita nostra brevis est,
> Brevi finietur.
> Venit mors velociter,
> Rapit nos atrociter.
> Nemini parcetur,
> Nemini parcetur.

Looking at the circle of fire, paying no attention to the crowd hanging back safely from the flames, he held up one hand. "Fear not, dear bibliophiles – these tomes are all mine." He took another match and lit it with a steady hand. He stood arms outstretched, closed his eyes and tipped his head skyward.

"Sincere apologies to Wagner and Wotan!"

Then he bent his right arm, touching the tiny flame to his soaking shirt.

All I could hear was screaming. It took a few moments before I realized the screams were my own.

Simon burst into my room.

"Lily?"

I sat up in bed, breathing hard, my heart hammering and covered in sweat. I hadn't had a nightmare that horrible since I was a child.

"I'm fine," I lied. "Sorry I woke you. Bad dream. Go back to bed."

"Are you sure? I can stay ..."

"I'm sure."

"Well, if you need me, just knock," he said and he closed my door. I heard him pad back to his room.

I tried but couldn't go back to sleep so I got up quietly, tossed on a robe and went to the computer. It was just after five in the morning.

It was obvious to me that Simon needed a change of focus and I needed to deal with my anxiety. My subconscious was giving me a message. I debated sharing my dream with Simon but thought that would only depress him more. Instead, that evening, I suggested a Thanksgiving dinner at my place for our trio.

"Thanks, El, but I have other plans," he said.

"Really?"

"You sound surprised."

"Well, I just thought ... you've been so ..."

"Despondent? Discouraged? Depressed?"

"Yes."

"It seems as though the cosmos is against me, but that's likely just the conspiracy diva in me speaking."

"I know it's tough."

"Builds character."

"So the pundits say," I said. "What is so bloody important that you can't come and break bread with your old landlady and your separated chum?"

"I've been given the opportunity to get away, spend some time in a secluded cabin in the woods. Leave everything behind. The place is quite rustic. No electricity or running water."

"What will you do up there?"

He sighed. "Read."

"What?"

"Oh, Lily, the past few months have been a huge distraction and disappointment. I want to get back to texts I've neglected for far too long."

"Can't they wait a bit longer?"

He shook his head. "I need some time alone to determine where I go from here. Just me and my beloved tomes."

"Are you sure?"

"Absolutely."

"If you change your mind or get tired of the primitive plumbing ..."

"I shall race back here to devour a drumstick and nibble your pumpkin pie."

When I told Greg, he said he understood.

"Why can't he just talk things out with us?"

"Guys aren't like that. Sometimes we just need to go back to our caves and be alone to figure things out. It's not about feelings. It's about solutions."

"Don't give me that primitive Neanderthal bullshit."

"Lil, you're a great friend, a good scholar, and a successful professional. But you're not a guy."

I rolled my eyes. "I'll never understand men."

"You don't have to. Let him go. When he gets back, I bet he'll have it all figured out. He is a genius you know."

"He never lets me forget it."

Simon left early in the morning on the Thursday before Thanksgiving. I saw him as I was getting ready to go off to work. He looked haggard. He had three bags packed, one with provisions and clothing and two filled with papers and books. When I asked him about the wisdom of taking so much to read, he said being alone five days, he didn't want to risk running out of material.

The temperature was unseasonably cool so he was wearing a tweed sport coat. When I saw him, I laughed.

"Is Mr. Chips going camping?"

"The very sight of me amuses you, does it?" he asked.

"You're the only person I know who would go up north wearing tweed. Don't you have a ski jacket?"

"I will not wear an anorak before it is time."

"I'm sure the squirrels will vote you Most Stylish Forest Dweller."

"El, I left you a little something. It's in my room on the night stand but don't open it until Gobble Gobble Day."

"You have my word," I said as I reached over to pull up his collar. "And you stay warm, eh? This is Canada, not England."

"I promise."

"Goodbye, Mr. Chips." I hugged him.

"Goodbye, El." He squeezed me tighter and he was off. I forgot to ask him how he was getting up north but then thought I was fussing far too much about a grown man.

Spending Thanksgiving with Greg was perfect. We talked, laughed, and flirted, too. It felt so good. I dared to think I was being given a second chance with him.

The phone rang while Greg and I were washing up after dinner. My hands were covered in suds so I asked Greg to pick it up in the other room. When he came back into the room, all colour had drained from his face.

"What's wrong?"

"The cabin … those papers and books … all of it went up in flames. Simon's dead."

CHAPTER 28

THE INVESTIGATORS CONCLUDED THE FIRE STARTED WITH A single candle. They also found two empty whiskey bottles. One idea was Simon had been drinking while reading by candlelight and fell asleep. The candle burned down to the nub in a ceramic holder that heated up and then exploded. With so much paper and wood, the blaze spread quickly. He would have little chance to escape.

Simon had rented a car to drive up to the cabin. He had left his wallet in the glove box, making it easier for the police to identify him and to ring me. Being Simon, he always kept his documents in order, and they found a slip of paper with my name, telephone number and address as his emergency contact.

I took a week off work to deal with everything. Greg was my rock. I couldn't stomach seeing what remained of the cabin so he picked up the rental car and drove it back to Toronto while I made arrangements for a memorial. We found a file in Simon's desk that contained his Will; he left everything to Greg and me and named me as executrix, "because it sounds suitably responsible and a tad kinky" he added in a note in the margin. He stipulated that he wished to be cremated and his ashes sprinkled somewhere appropriate in Oxford. There were also instructions on dealing with his Newton manuscript, a copy of which we found on the corner of his nightstand.

Simon wasn't religious so we had a simple, non-denominational service in the university chapel. Friends and colleagues came from Boston, Manchester and Oxford as well as from India, Australia and Germany. Jean-Marc came over, too. If anyone doubted how Simon was loved, they only had to see the chapel, full of those bewildered by his death.

I couldn't believe he was gone. It took me a month before I could clean out his room even though it was in my condo. One rainy Saturday, I decided it was time. I managed to hold myself together until I opened his closet door and found his college scarf hanging neatly on a hook. I buried my face in it to get a hint of Simon's cologne. So many memories flashed through my mind as tears poured down my cheeks. After what seemed like an eternity, I carefully folded it up and took it back to my room, where I put it away in my cedar chest.

Later that same weekend Greg came over to help. He handed me the envelope Simon had mentioned just before he went up north for Thanksgiving. I'd seen it on the night stand but was too raw to read it before.

"Are you ready now?" Greg asked.

I nodded. My hands were shaking as I opened the flap. I sat down on the bed, and Greg sat beside me as I read the note.

"Dearest Lily:

I am a coward. I cannot bring myself to face you because, for the first time in my life, words fail me.

For all of my achievements and all of my successes, the greatest triumph has been an accidental one – having you as a steadfast and true friend is the one single constant that has sustained me. I had naïvely believed that books or learning would be my truest companions. I was wrong. In the face of loss, whether loss of position, loss of love, or loss of direction, your faith in me has never wavered.

I shall never be able to express my gratitude for all that you have done for me. This weekend is a celebration of Thanksgiving and so I thank you, El. I confess that being this vulnerable frightens me but it would be obscenely remiss of me not to express my feelings and, therefore, I do so in writing.

Now I must go off to contemplate my future. I need to be worthy of your continued respect and your friendship. Whatever path I may take must be a true one.

Happy gobbling with Greg. Remember – nibble, don't bite!

Finally, in honour of the academic setting of where we first met, I shall sing a chorus or two of *Gaudemus igitur* as I celebrate this day of giving thanks because, as the song goes, '*Vita nostra brevis est*'. Enough said.

Humbly and affectionately,

Simon."

Greg held me as I sobbed. I let him read the letter and we made a promise to take Simon's cremains to Oxford in the spring. When Greg left the next morning, I looked up the words to that song. The alternate title was *De Brevitate Vitae* or 'On the Shortness of Life'. Tears streamed down my face as I read the English translation of that stanza. It was the same one Simon sang in my dream:

> Our life is brief
> Soon it will end.
> Death comes quickly
> Snatches us cruelly
> No one shall be spared.

I never told a soul about my dream. Not even Greg. I still wonder if, in the end, Simon had truly been master of his own destiny. If he had to die, I would have rather he died like he did in my dream: forcefully, eloquently, publicly. He could have made the world see that something was dreadfully wrong, not with him but with academia.

All Simon had tried to do in the end was to find work, any work. Instead, he died shrouded in ignominy, alone but for the ambiguously accusatory presence of whisky bottles. No one knew his despair at becoming just another disposable academic.

Months later, I was still seething with anger, at Simon, at the system, at those who denied there was a problem, but I was too cowardly to rail at anyone but my lovers and friends. My life would plod along because I gave up on my dream. Simon's life ended because he stubbornly refused to give up on his destiny.

Simon's death meant something far greater than whatever happened in that cabin, but sadly, only to me.

ACKNOWLEDGMENTS

THIS IDEA FOR THIS BOOK HAS BEEN WITH ME FOR YEARS. WHEN I finally began to write, I realized the challenge that lay before me. I would like to acknowledge those who quietly inspired, encouraged and supported me in taking the characters from my imagination to the page.

Joan Thomas, my instructor in the Banff Centre's 'Writing with Style' program taught me about clarity and voice. Joan and my Banff workshop colleagues -- Hali Ahlfeld, Nina Levitt, Dana Robinson, Natalie Sampson, Nancy Sayre, Valerie Scott, and Charles Wiseman -- were the first to read excerpts of this work and offer cogent critiques.

Frieda Wishinsky, my instructor at the Humber School for Writers Summer Workshop, taught me much about crisp, clear writing and encouraged me to write fiction.

Fellow writer and Humber workshop colleague Eric Murphy is the finest example of tenacity and attention to craft; he is also a gracious host and a steadfast friend. Writing is a solitary art and Eric understands the need to step away from the computer to talk about the latest draft and the importance of good wine and cheese. Will

O'Hara is a gentle soul who, like Eric, offered up his experience in publishing fiction as a guide for me. Marc Stevens was an inspiration, too, and understands better than most the effort that goes into writing a book.

Ceilidh Marlow and the editing and design team at FriesenPress made the publishing process a pleasure. Natasha Clark is a marketing maven. Designer Matthew Ross of Springfed Creative spent a morning with me on a 'shoot' and is responsible for the evocative cover photograph.

Steve Walton started this journey with me, served as my 'road map', and after all these years, remains a true friend. Like all my fellow grad students and postdoctoral colleagues, he knows the twists, turns and precipices on the academic path, but he faces each one with a grace that I will always admire.

Zack and Olivia Reid, my nephew and niece, inspire me to create and to write, carrying on from my mother, Leona Fedunkiw, who instilled in me a passion for storytelling.

Finally, I must acknowledge three men who, each in their own way, 'chivvied' me along to complete this novel. John Rammell, a wonderful writer and kind soul, is my touchstone for quality. George Dutton knows the characters in this novel better than anyone, having shared litres of café coffee as I discussed the story, reading chapters as they were written and giving honest feedback that only made the book better. Finally, I thank my husband Bert Hall, who has been insidiously directing me to "put it in the book" for years.

CPSIA information can be obtained at www.ICGtesting.com
Printed in the USA
LVOW08s0122280114

371169LV00001B/18/P

9 781460 233801